**"Will you hold me for a little while, Brett?"
Leah asked.**

"Now?" He sat motionless, trying to conceal his hunger for any contact she would allow.

She nodded. "You make me feel safe," she said softly. "I need to feel safe."

He piled the pillows against the headboard and drew Leah into his arms.

She turned to him and rested her head on his bare shoulder. He responded instantly, his nerve endings igniting, his muscles tensing beneath her fingertips.

"Are we lovers, Brett?"

He felt shock pummel his senses like a fighter gone mad in the ring. "No, Leah, we're not lovers." *We haven't been for a long time, but it isn't because I don't want you every second of every day.*

"Then why do I want you every time you touch me? . . ."

WHAT ARE *LOVESWEPT* ROMANCES?

They are stories of true romance and touching emotion. We believe those two very important ingredients are constants in our highly sensual and very believable stories in the *LOVESWEPT* line. Our goal is to give you, the reader, stories of consistently high quality that may sometimes make you laugh, sometimes make you cry, but are always fresh and creative and contain many delightful surprises within their pages.

Most romance fans read an enormous number of books. Those they truly love, they keep. Others may be traded with friends and soon forgotten. We hope that each *LOVESWEPT* romance will be a treasure—a "keeper." We will always try to publish

LOVE STORIES YOU'LL NEVER FORGET
BY AUTHORS YOU'LL ALWAYS REMEMBER

The Editors

Loveswept 600

Laura Taylor
Just Friends

BANTAM BOOKS

NEW YORK · TORONTO · LONDON · SYDNEY · AUCKLAND

JUST FRIENDS

A Bantam Book / March 1993

If you would be interested in receiving protective vinyl
covers for your Loveswept books, please write to this address
for information:

Loveswept
Bantam Books
P.O. Box 985
Hicksville, NY 11802

ISBN 0-553-44367-4

Published simultaneously in the United States and Canada

PRINTED IN THE UNITED STATES OF AMERICA

OPM   0 9 8 7 6 5 4 3 2 1

For Toni,
supportive sister, loving mother, and skilled aviator

One

The woman moaned as she shifted restlessly atop the examining table. Her thoughts resembling a tangled clump of yarn, she sensed that she was in the throes of the worst migraine of her life. She gingerly moved her head, but the brass band playing in her skull grew so deafening that she exhaled raggedly and let herself go limp.

She flinched when she heard a deep voice mutter a harsh-sounding word. A heartbeat later she felt the possessive grip of what could only be a strong male hand as it encompassed her smaller one.

She struggled to open her eyes and succeeded in squinting up at the man who stood beside her. Glimpsing the worry etched into his rugged features, she experienced a moment of genuine panic.

"What . . ." she began, trying once again to lift her head. Made dizzy by her efforts, she sank back down.

"Take it easy. You're going to be all right," he promised.

"Don't . . . lie," she pleaded as trumpets blared

and drums pounded out a furious beat within her skull. "Tell . . . what . . . happened." She squeezed her eyes shut. Trembling, she clung to his hand and drifted on a sea of pure agony.

Brett Upton couldn't take his eyes off Leah Holbrook. He realized that the years—years they'd spent apart—had enhanced her delicate beauty. Although pale and bruised from the kidnapping attempt he'd managed to foil, Leah continued to represent every memory of love he possessed. She'd also become his personal symbol of light and hope in the midst of the darkness and chaos that dominated his world.

Amazed even now by the warm, silky feel of her skin, Brett stroked the inside of her arm in an attempt to soothe her. The knowledge that she had been hurt because of him ate at his soul, and he silently vowed that no further harm would come to her. He would protect her. With his life, if need be.

Footsteps sounded in the hallway. Brett glanced up, his hand sliding automatically to the weapon tucked against the small of his back. Concealed from view beneath his leather jacket, the gun was part and parcel of the dark side of his life. When the doctor who'd examined Leah and then ordered a series of X rays stepped into view, Brett let his hand fall away from the gun.

"How's our patient doing?"

The patient winced in reaction to the unfamiliar, highly pitched female voice, then brought a hand up to massage her temple. She groaned when she made contact with a walnut-sized lump just above her hairline.

Brett carefully smoothed Leah's hand away from her wound, clenching his fist when he saw the droplets of blood that still dotted her forehead beneath wispy golden bangs. But he managed to answer the doctor's question with a steady voice. "She's awake, but she's still groggy and in a lot of pain."

"That's not surprising, Mr. Upton," observed the doctor, sliding a sheaf of X rays onto a nearby table. "She slammed head on into a slab of concrete when she fell. Just be thankful she's no longer unconscious, because that would certainly be cause for concern."

"Does she need to be hospitalized?" Brett asked.

"I don't believe that will be necessary."

"What about the X rays?" he asked, his voice as hard as granite as he prepared himself for the worst.

"Good news on that score. I've studied them, and I don't see any abnormalities."

Brett exhaled, his relief obvious.

"Head . . . hurts," Leah whimpered. She opened aquamarine-colored eyes swimming with tears, peered up at the doctor, and pleaded, with a wounded look, for relief.

The doctor patted her shoulder. "Of course it hurts, my dear, but your headache should be gone by morning."

Feeling responsible for what had happened to Leah, and frustrated by it, Brett demanded, "Can't you give her something for the pain?" He took Leah's hand and held it tightly.

"I could, Mr. Upton, but I'd rather not. It's best not to drug a patient with a head injury, but something tells me you already realize that, don't you?"

He nodded, the gentleness in the doctor's voice shaming him. He didn't have to like it, but his experience on the battlefield and his first-aid training assured him that the doctor was right. Brett also knew that Leah was strong enough to get through until morning on sheer grit if she had to. Although he'd purposely kept his distance from her, he'd spent the last six years acquiring a healthy respect for her courage, so he didn't expect her to cave in on him now.

"I do empathize with your concern for your friend, but unless she experiences bouts of dizziness, blurred vision, or recurring headaches, she should be just fine. I do expect you to keep a very close eye on her, though." The doctor made a final note in Leah's file before closing it and placing it atop the X rays. "Now, I believe you mentioned something about packing for a vacation in the Pacific Northwest when Miss Holbrook fell."

"We can cancel the trip," he said, concealing his desire to remain on the move in order to guarantee Leah's safety.

"Actually I'd advise you to go ahead with your plans," the doctor remarked, "but keep the schedule light and undemanding for the first forty-eight hours or so. Miss Holbrook needs plenty of rest and relaxation right now, and she shouldn't have to deal with stress of any kind."

He commented, "She does need a break."

"I do?" she whispered. *From what?* she wondered, feeling both vulnerable and disoriented.

Not knowing how to deal with the violent images of angry-faced men wielding knives and guns that filled her mind each time she closed her eyes, she concentrated instead on the strength of the callused, long-fingered hand still gripping hers. She found comfort in his touch, although some deep-seated instinct told her that his sturdy hands were capable of things other than reassurance.

"There's also the very real possibility that she won't ever remember her fall," the doctor was saying, "and she may experience other memory lapses, but don't be alarmed unless the situation persists for more than a few days. I trust you won't hesitate to take Miss Holbrook to a hospital should she experience any unusual changes in her motor skills."

"Of course not, Doctor."

Brett fervently hoped that Leah would never remember the men who'd tried to kidnap her because of their vendetta against him, but he suspected she would. And then she would blame him for what had happened. He knew he deserved her anger, and was prepared to accept it.

"I . . . feel . . . invisible," Leah muttered through gritted teeth. "Want to . . . get up. Now."

The doctor smiled sympathetically and patted her shoulder again. Brett's guilt flashed in his eyes, but he didn't say a word. What could he say? he wondered. How did a man apologize to a woman for placing her life in jeopardy?

Leah pushed herself upright to a seated position. When the doctor made no attempt to stop her, Brett glanced at the older woman, an obvious question in his eyes. She shook her head in warning and returned her gaze to Leah, watching her with an intensity that suggested she was evaluating her patient's efforts from a strictly medical perspective.

Leah heard the discordant blare of trumpets in her head as she sat there and tried to catch her breath. She suddenly swayed to one side. Strong hands reached out to steady her.

A full minute ticked by on the wall clock behind the doctor. And then another. Gritting her teeth, she slid off the examining table. She felt as though someone had pitched her off the side of a steep cliff. Her legs crumpled beneath her, but Brett grabbed her before she hit the floor.

She smothered a cry of surprise when he wrapped his arms around her. She inhaled his musky male scent, felt the sturdiness of his solid thighs, lean hips, and flat belly, and willingly accepted the haven provided by his encompassing embrace. Her senses swam, and her pulse fluctuated madly.

"Doctor . . ." Brett began, his voice sharp with alarm.

"She's fine. Just let her get her bearings, Mr. Upton."

"What . . . happened . . . to me?" she asked as her head started to clear.

His expression strained, Brett glanced down at her. "We can talk later."

"You apparently fell on the sidewalk in front of your home while you were packing for a trip, but I don't want you to worry—you haven't done any lasting damage to yourself," supplied the doctor before she gave Brett a stern look. "Don't coddle her, Mr. Upton, and always answer her questions. Her reactions will help you gauge her awareness of the world around her. That's going to be particularly important during the next few days."

He nodded, his jaw tightening as he ground his teeth together.

Leah, who peered up at him with undisguised curiosity, frowned as she studied his hard-featured face. The worry in his expression confused her. He actually seemed to care about her well-being. She wondered why.

"How do you feel?" His tone of voice was roughly intimate.

She rolled her eyes, her weak laugh turning almost instantly into a groan. "Don't . . . ask."

"You feel as though a marching band has taken up residence in your head, don't you, my dear?" the doctor said.

She nodded, then wished she hadn't. Her brains felt even more scrambled, her head throbbed fiercely, and the tenderness of her ribs and hip hinted at having been flogged. "Something for . . . the pain, please?" she asked hopefully.

"I truly sympathize with your discomfort, but I'm very reluctant to prescribe painkillers. You're better off sleeping through the night without any articifical assistance. You've got contusions along your rib cage and right hip, and I expect they'll become quite colorful over the next few weeks, but they'll fade with time." The doctor tugged a penlight from her pocket, took Leah's chin in hand, and said, "Focus on the light for me."

She cooperated, but the effort involved exacerbated the pain in her head.

"Very good. Now follow my finger with your eyes."

She again did as instructed. The doctor finally turned off the penlight and slipped it back into the breast pocket of her lab coat.

Leah closed her eyes, seeking a refuge from the intense pain. She found it as she burrowed into Brett's arms. Focusing on the warmth and security he provided, she barely heard the doctor's next comment.

"You two can be on your way now. When you get back from your vacation, let me know how you're feeling."

She felt like a drunken sailor as Brett escorted her out of the examining room and down a long hallway. Resting her head against his shoulder, she kept her eyes closed as much as possible as they walked. Even blinking hurt.

They paused briefly at the reception area while Brett paid the bill, then he guided Leah out of the small Monterey community medical clinic. He paused just beyond the front doors and scanned the poorly lighted parking lot with the intensity of a hunter. When she swayed, he tightened his hold on her and urged, "Lean on me."

"I already . . . am."

"Yeah," he muttered, leading her to a bench. "Wait here while I get the car."

She grabbed his hands. "Don't leave me," she whispered, a rush of panic and pain nearly overcoming her. "Please."

Her fear startled him. He drew her into the shelter of his arms, one hand cupping the back of her head, the other fixed firmly at her waist. "Relax. I'm not going anywhere without you," he said, knowing he'd rather die than abandon her ever again.

She lifted her head from his hard chest and looked up at him. Unshed tears glittered in her eyes. "I can . . . keep up. Really."

Ignoring all the caution flags waving in his mind, he leaned down and pressed his lips to her forehead. "I believe you. You're the most stubborn woman I've ever known."

Stubborn? She blinked in confusion.

Brett smiled at her then, a tender, regret-filled smile. Fascinated by the change in his features, Leah tilted her head and studied him.

Absently touching the sides of his face with her fingertips, she completely forgot that staring was rude and that touching without invitation was even ruder. She gently traced his high cheekbones and his square jaw, but hesitated when she reached his lips. Her fingertips lingered at the corners of his mouth, the sensual shape of his lips mesmerizing her. She sighed, the sound tremulous.

Brett turned and pressed his lips to her fingertips, his hot breath bathing her skin. She jerked in shock, then experienced a sudden flash of lucidity. She realized little could ease the harshness of the angular lines and strong bones of his face, but that sometimes an unexpected smile would soften that ferocity and make him less dangerous-looking.

"Ready?" he asked, glancing once again across the parking lot.

"Yes." Her headache returned with a vengeance the instant she moved, but she knew she had no choice. Standing on the sidewalk in front of the medical clinic for the remainder of the night wasn't an option.

She appreciated the supportive arm he slipped around her waist before they stepped off the curb together and slowly crossed the parking lot. When she stumbled, Brett caught her and lifted her up into his arms.

"Better?" he asked, his breath ruffling the wispy bangs at her forehead.

"Much." She closed her eyes and gingerly massaged her temples as she huddled against his chest. "Safer too," she murmured, not giving a moment's thought to her remark.

His heartbeat stilled, and he frowned. "Safer?"

Tires squealed nearby. Brett stiffened, then turned abruptly to search the darkness for the source of the sound.

Brett's sudden movement sent a laserlike shaft of pain into the center of Leah's skull. She started to protest, but her words died unspoken when he surged forward into a teeth-jarring jog across the parking lot. The unexpected flash of headlights bore down on them as she heard the furious sound of a highly revved truck engine and the squeal of tires.

"Hold on to me!" Brett shouted as he hurled their bodies through the air.

They landed atop the hood of a parked car, Brett

managing to cushion her fall with his body. He swiftly rolled over and, sprawled across her, he reached for his gun.

She felt the impact right down to her soul when the truck slammed into their perch. She clutched at Brett, her fingers digging into his shoulders, her face pressed against his neck as he crouched over her, and her scream of fear trapped in her throat.

Brett's physical strength and his determination to protect Leah kept them atop the hood when the truck slammed into them a second time. He fired several rounds into the windshield of the vehicle, and someone shrieked with pain. The truck hurriedly backed up, tires squealing once again as it exited the parking lot at high speed.

Brett, gathering Leah into his arms, felt an unexpected rush of arousal streak into his veins. With his hips lodged between her parted thighs and his chest pressed against her high, full breasts, he remembered the volatile passion they'd once shared—and the intervening six years, empty years filled with violence and secondhand stories about her life.

Breathless and trembling, she closed her eyes and held her head with both hands. When she could finally speak, she muttered, "Blasted . . . drunk . . . drivers."

Forgive me, he begged silently as he held her, *forgive me for making you vulnerable to men who seek deadly retribution for my actions.*

Shoving his gun into the front waistband of his jeans, Brett didn't tell Leah that the men in the truck were terrorists, not drunks. She wasn't in any shape to absorb the reality of the situation, he told himself, but his conscience twitched and cautioned him to be more honest with himself. He feared her reaction to the truth.

Brett rolled off her, his body starving, as it had been for six years, for her gentle touch and fiery passion. He consciously forced himself to forget the desire enflaming his senses and tightening the fit of his jeans.

Drawing in a steadying breath, he eased Leah off the car's hood, draped his jacket over her shoulders, and then quickly carried her the remaining distance to his rental car. He jerked open the passenger door, ignoring the shouted questions coming from the people clustered at the front doors of the clinic. All he cared about was getting Leah to a safe place.

"I don't understand . . . you actually seem . . . to care about me," she managed to gasp as she slipped her arms around his waist and rested her spinning head against his chest.

Brett flinched. He fought a silent but fierce battle to keep his emotions in check as he freed himself from her grasp, tucked her into the car, and hurriedly fastened her seatbelt. "Of course, I care," he ground out, although not surprised that Leah would question both his actions and his motives.

Kneeling beside her, Brett hesitated when he noted her baffled expression and the way she stared first at his gun and then up at his face. He reached out and covered her hand with his. Despite the chill night air, her skin was warm. "Leah . . ." he began.

She shook her head slowly, as though to clear her thoughts. He fell silent, his dark eyes reflecting his concern for her.

"Understand. Just . . . doing your . . . job, aren't you?"

Brett exhaled, the harsh sound bursting free of his body to disturb the stillness of the silent parking lot. Fighting the urge to confess that he'd lied all those years ago when he'd told her that he hadn't loved her enough to marry her, he released her hand and got to his feet. He shut the door and raced around to the opposite side of the car.

He didn't blame Leah for believing that she was just another task to be dealt with and resolved. Six years ago he'd put his career in Naval Intelligence ahead of a life with her. No matter the motive for his decision, he'd wounded her. She obviously hadn't forgiven him, and he didn't blame her. He hadn't forgiven himself.

Brett also knew that their tumultuous personal history, not just his absence from her life when she'd needed him most, would always fail to inspire trust or anything remotely close to confidence in his ability to protect her.

She sank back against the seat, Brett's leather jacket dwarfing her body as she huddled beneath it. While he started the car and drove out of the parking lot, she waged a short, futile war against the fatigue that enveloped her like a dense fog. She failed to register the wail of police sirens in the distance or the diminishing streetlights that signaled their departure from Monterey. Slumping sideways, she descended into a fuzzy world of twilight sleep filled with unanswered questions that darted around in her mind like annoying insects.

"Why are you so worried about me?"

"Are we friends?"

"Are you taking me home?"

"Do you know where I live?"

"Why can't I remember my name?"

Two

As he drove from Monterey to San Francisco, Brett kept a close eye on Leah while she slept. He also watched for any hint that they were being followed. After three hours of being on the road he concluded that the men who were after Leah were keeping their distance. But certain that they would back off only temporarily, Brett knew he would have to remain guarded.

He deliberately selected a well-known San Francisco hotel as their destination. He reasoned that the best way to blend into a crowded city was to go to a highly visible location and bide their time. Brett decide that they would play the role of vacationers who simply needed a heavy dose of R and R.

He also realized that Leah deserved and needed time to recuperate before he explained their situation. He wanted her strong, even if it meant earning her anger. He needed her, once she understood the crisis they faced, to work with him, not against him. That, he knew, would be the tricky part, because Leah would have to trust his judgment and his instincts, something she would be reluctant to do.

Brett pulled up in front of the hotel, an enormous, multistoried glass-and-stone structure situated at the edge of San Francisco's financial district and less than a block from the fabled bay. Cabs were lined up on one side of the driveway despite the late hour, the drivers either dozing or reading. Brett noted a well-dressed couple returning from an evening out, a police cruiser that had paused at a red light at the next intersection, and two hotel bellmen who stood near the double-door entrance to the registration area of the hotel.

Since nothing appeared out of the ordinary, he raised his hand and signaled one of the bellmen. The young man jogged over and took the key to the trunk from Brett.

Turning to Leah, who had huddled against him, he gathered her even closer and held her. Although still asleep, she slipped her arms around his waist and tucked her face against his neck. Brett sighed raggedly, aware that her trust would soon evaporate.

He felt self-indulgent as he stole a few quite moments with her in his arms. He inhaled the seductive scent of white ginger, his body responding to the memories he attached to the fragrance. Surprised that she still wore it, he recalled giving the perfume to her as a gift following a trip to the Orient. Pressing his lips against her temple, Brett took care not to venture too close to the head wound she'd sustained during the attempted kidnapping. He felt her burrow closer, then go very still in his arms. Easing back, he found her staring up at him, an expression of confusion on her face.

"We're here," he explained as he struggled to keep his emotions and growing arousal under control. "Do you think you can walk on your own, or should I carry you?"

Reaching up, she used her fingertips to smooth away the frown lines that marred his forehead and made deep grooves on either side of his mouth. "What's wrong?"

Surprised that she would touch him once more with such gentleness, he couldn't conceal the shock that flashed in his eyes. "Nothing."

Leah looked even more confused. "Aren't I supposed to touch you?" she asked sleepily.

That she would feel the need to ask such a question made his heart plummet and reminded him of his cruel denial of his love for her six years ago. He gently covered her hand with his own, brought her fingers to his mouth, and pressed his lips against them.

She smiled, a tentative little smile that made his soul ache. The bewilderment that lingered in her blue-green eyes worried him, but he didn't know how to make it go away. "It's late," he remarked, even though he didn't want the moment or their closeness to end. "We need to get inside."

Leah nodded. Brett got out of the car and circled around the front of it, his eyes narrowed as he scanned the driveway for anything or anyone capable of posing a threat to Leah. He pulled open the passenger door, collected her shoulder bag from the floor behind the passenger seat, and gave it to her. Although he noticed her curiosity when she took a moment to study it, he didn't question her behavior. Instead he kept scanning the entrance to the hotel as he waited for her to scoot across the seat and out of the car.

Brett cautioned himself against reading anything into Leah's willingness to accept his extended hand or in her inclination to remain close to his side as they entered the hotel, paused to register at the front desk, and then boarded the penthouse elevator.

Certain that she would be her old feisty self again by morning, he chalked up her behavior to fatigue and to the emotional vulnerability brought on by her severe headache.

He watched her lean back against the mirrored elevator wall. Her quiet sigh served to emphasize her exhaustion, as did the shadows beneath her large eyes and the paleness of her already fair skin. His gaze grew openly possessive and hungry when she closed her eyes and rubbed her forehead with her fingertips. He looked away, the reminder that she'd been hurt because of him unnecessary, but he still couldn't escape their mirrored reflections.

He saw their images everywhere he looked, and he stopped trying to ignore the contrast between her pale skin and golden hair and his dark features and collar-length black hair. Although he considered Leah petite and fragile, she often reminded him of a brilliant sunburst on a cloudless day. In truth they were as different as night and day.

Brett knew that his large body and less-than-refined physical attributes, courtesy of his mother's Mediterranean heritage, made it possible for him to slip into the deadlier enclaves of both European and Middle Eastern terrorist factions. A woman he'd encountered a few years earlier had once called him Satan's issue when he'd spurned her attentions. He couldn't help thinking now that she'd been right on target with her observation, because he existed in a dark world filled with treachery and violence.

The elevator stopped abruptly, jarring him from his thoughts. Brett positioned himself so that he exited the elevator first. After glancing up and down the hallway, he drew Leah forward and kept his arm around her as they made their way to the end of the hall. He noticed that the bellman, per his instructions to the desk clerk, had deposited their luggage in the sitting room of their suite and departed.

Brett locked and bolted the door. Pocketing his keys, he asked, "How about something to eat before we call it a night?"

Leah paused near the stack of suitcases in the center of the elegantly furnished room. "Please, but nothing heavy. Perhaps some soup or a salad."

Leaning down, she studied the name tags on two of the bags. Leah Holbrook, they said. She vaguely remembered someone calling her Leah at the clinic. She also noticed that the third piece of luggage, a black leather carryon, was untagged. She straightened, her eyes repeatedly straying to Brett as she wandered around the spacious sitting room.

She watched and listened as he picked up the phone and asked the operator to ring room service. After giving their order, he recradled the receiver. "Be right back," he promised.

Brett disappeared without another word, swiftly checking the layout and potential security problems of the suite's bedrooms and bathrooms, finding a window that needed to be secured, and then returning to the sitting room a few minutes later.

Leah, seated on the sofa, shrugged out of his leather jacket just as he walked back into the room. Her expression intent, she inspected the contents of the purse he'd handed her earlier. She considered the wallet the most logical place to start as she tried to cope with her mounting anxiety.

What's my name? she asked herself as she unsnapped the wallet and flipped it open. *What is my name?*

"Leah?" he said, as though in response to her silent question.

Startled, she glanced up at him. Gripping the

wallet she'd found with both hands until her knuckles turned white, she smothered the apprehension threatening to overwhelm her by the sheer force of her will. "Yes?"

"Need anything?" he asked.

She shivered and thought, *Just an encapsulated version of my life.* "Not at the moment," Leah lied, putting on a brave front when all she wanted to do was crawl into his arms and be held until her fear retreated and she recalled her name.

Brett crossed the room and paused in front of the French doors that led out onto the suite's balcony. Leah used the time to study him as he tested the sturdiness of the locks. Broad-shouldered, narrow-hipped, and long-legged, he had the body of an athlete who trained regularly.

She saw that his gun was still wedged into the back waistband of his jeans. He seemed unaware of it, and Leah concluded that carrying a weapon was part of his everyday life. She also decided that it suited his manner, which was that of a man who insisted on total control of his environment, not just the people in it.

Although she suspected that he was a cop, she thought his hair seemed a bit long for someone in law enforcement. She assumed that he worked undercover. An unexpected thought entered her mind then, making her wonder if she'd broken the law. She immediately rejected the notion, because she knew on some instinctive level that she wasn't a criminal. She met his gaze when he turned to look at her, and Leah viewed once again the strong lines of his hard-featured face and the almost fathomless darkness of his eyes.

The structure of his face provoked a vague memory of a painting she'd seen at some point in her life.

The artist had captured her subject with boldly aggressive strokes. Leah sensed that this man was bold and aggressive, but he also reassured her in an odd, indefinable way. He made her feel safe, but he also made her insides soften when he looked at her.

There was a hint of sensual knowledge in the sweep of his gaze. Were they lovers? she wondered suddenly. He'd touched her like a lover. She imagined for a moment what intimacy between them might be like, and the passionate images that filled her mind amazed her. Her thoughts sent heat rushing into her veins as she stared back at him in the silence of the sitting room.

Looking feverish, Leah glanced back down at the wallet, which contained a California driver's license, several credit cards, and a few photographs. Even though her head still hurt and her senses were in an uproar, she felt stronger and more coherent than she had in several hours. But with her clarity of thought came unpleasant truths she knew she couldn't avoid—she didn't know this man, and she had no idea what had happened to her.

Brett flicked a glance at his watch as he sank into the chair positioned opposite the sofa. "The food should be here soon."

Leah tried to smile, but she simply succeeded in looking strained.

"How do you feel?"

"Tired," she admitted.

"The doctor—"

"—was right. My head still hurts, but it's not as bad now."

"Something's on your mind, love. Talk to me, why don't you? You can trust me."

Love? She rolled the word around in her mind, trying it on for size and subsequently discovering that it didn't sound totally foreign to her. Still, she didn't like the generic quality of it. Leah abruptly abandoned her perch on the edge of the sofa cushion and wandered in the direction of the French doors.

She paused at the closed beveled-glass doors. Her blurred image stared back at her. She didn't acknowledge Brett, even though he followed her and closed the drapes. Nor did she resist when he put his arm around her and led her away from the French doors.

Leah felt a sudden stab of annoyance that he was being so solicitous, but she didn't understand why. Slipping free of him halfway across the room, she turned and faced him. "Can I really trust you?"

"With your life."

Leah blinked in surprise because he sounded as though he'd just taken a vow. She saw his sincerity in the depths of his dark eyes, in the determined expression etched into his face, and in the rigidity of his large body. She extended her hand, the license resting in her upturned palm.

Brett accepted her offering, his gaze narrowing as he glanced first at the license and then back at Leah. "What's wrong?"

"As you can see, it says my name is Leah Holbrook. It also gives my address. Why are we in a San Francisco hotel if I live in Monterey? Why didn't you just take me home?"

Leah searched his face for some telltale emotion. She thought she saw a flash of surprise, but he quickly concealed his reaction to her question behind an enigmatic expression that worried her. Maybe she *had* done something illegal.

"Love . . ."

Leah flinched. "Don't call me that, please."

Brett returned the driver's license and then

shoved his fingers through his dense black hair. A heavy strand drifted back across his forehead almost immediately. "You always did hate it." Shoving both hands into the back pockets of his jeans, he remained in the middle of the room.

"I guess I still do." She edged away from him until the backs of her knees bumped against the sofa. She sank down onto the center cushion. "Until I saw the luggage tags and the driver's license, I didn't know my name. If Leah Holbrook even is my name."

Brett briefly went as still as a stone statue. "The doctor said your memory might be a little spotty for a day or two, but that once you've had a chance to rest, whatever memory gaps you're experiencing are sure to disappear."

"Gaps?" She laughed, the sound short and filled with incredulity. "You're not listening to me. I definitely have gaps. Thirty years worth of gaps, according to the date of birth on this driver's license. We are not just talking 'spotty.' We're talking amnesia, or some form of it, because I can't remember *anything*," she insisted, her tone brittle as the temper she didn't even know she had flared to life.

"I thought you meant you didn't remember the trip, but you're . . ." His voice trailed off.

"I'm talking about my life, not a trip. What if I never remember who I am?" she asked, real fear in her voice.

"You will."

"How can you be so sure?"

"I just am. I've seen this kind of thing before."

"Am I under arrest?"

"Of course not!"

Her hand went to her temple. "Please, don't shout at me."

Brett muttered an ugly, totally self-directed

phrase under his breath. "You're a little confused right now. It's not surprising. You really smacked your head when you fell."

"Tell me about it, please."

"Leah, this conversation can wait. You're tired and hungry."

"But not deaf or stupid. Tell me what's happened. Now," she insisted as she struggled to stay calm. His obvious reluctance to talk to her heightened her tension. "I'm frightened."

Brett started pacing. "You don't remember any aspect of your life?"

"That's what I just said."

"You don't remember anything at all?" he clarified. He caught himself before he asked, *Don't you remember our son?*

He watched her shake her head and send her long golden hair on an evocative journey across her shoulders and down her back. Brett slowly approached her, his body language as unthreatening as he could make it. Going down on one knee in front of Leah, he smoothed his hand up and down her arm with the same gentleness he would've used on a small, injured animal.

When she looked at him, he saw tears of pain, confusion, and fatigue welling in her eyes, but he managed not to draw her into his arms. He had to set the tone of their relationship quickly, he reminded himself. He'd reentered her life to protect her when an informant alerted him to the death threats against Leah and her child, not to beg for a second chance at what he'd so foolishly given up.

Six years ago he'd told himself that he was protecting her by not exposing her to the jeopardy of being married to someone in his line of work. He'd done the honorable thing then, but that hadn't lessened his loneliness or his desire for her. And in spite of his efforts the people he'd wanted to save her from had finally succeeded in harming her. He knew they wouldn't stop until she and the boy were dead.

Brett's thoughts raced at top speed. Although he knew he couldn't keep her ignorant indefinitely about the terrorist threat, he realized that the task of protecting her would be far less complicated if he had the power to insulate her from the reality of their situation during their stay in San Francisco and while in transit to Seattle.

He knew, too, that Leah deserved his help as she tried to regain her memory. He intended to aid her in restoring it, but slowly and with great care. Even more crucial was the fact that she deserved his protection from an enemy she didn't even know she had, an enemy intent on directing his wrath against innocents like Leah and her five-and-a-half-year-old son, thanks to his discovery of her link to both Brett Upton and Micah Holbrook, the men who'd designed his impending downfall. With any kind of luck and with the help of European law enforcement authorities, Micah had already begun arresting members of the terrorist faction.

As well, Brett felt reluctant to increase her anxiety about the well-being of a child she didn't remember at the moment. He knew the boy and Leah's parents were on their way to a safe house, thanks to the security personnel he'd ordered to Seattle, where Leah's son was spending his Easter holiday. He would protect Leah while her older brother, Micah Holbrook, who was also his closest friend and the commanding officer of a second covert counterterrorism team operated by Naval Intelligence, handled the roundup of the terrorist group responsible for multiple bombings at naval installations around the globe, not just the vengeance-prompted death threats against Leah and her child.

"Please talk to me," she whispered.

He exhaled harshly and refocused on her. "Shall I start at the beginning?"

"Please."

"I'd just arrived. I saw you putting your luggage into the trunk of your car. It was dark, and you must've tripped on the curb. I wasn't close enough to catch you before you fell and hit your head on the cement."

Two men were trying to wrestle you to the ground, he remembered, *but you tried to fight them off. I was running toward you, shouting your name like a crazy man. I couldn't use my gun, because I was afraid you'd get caught in the cross fire. One of the men shoved you when he spotted me coming at him, and you fell. I heard you cry out just before your head hit the pavement. At first I thought they'd killed you. I wanted to die, too, but only after I'd made them pay for what they'd done to you.*

Brett gripped her hand, unaware that he was on the verge of crushing her fingers. "You scared the life out of me when I couldn't wake you up."

"You took me to the clinic?"

"Of course."

"You were holding my hand then too," she remarked. "I felt safe when you held my hand."

"Why didn't you tell the doctor you couldn't remember anything?" he asked.

"Would it have made a difference? I don't think there's a pill for this particular malady. Besides, I hardly even remember the clinic, let alone the doctor, although I'm almost positive I said something to you after we got into the car."

"You were mumbling in your sleep," he recalled. "I

should have paid more attention to what you were saying."

"That's all right. You couldn't have known." She paused and glanced down at their entwined fingers. "Who exactly are you?"

"Brett Matthew Upton." *Commander, United States Navy. The man who loves you. The father of your son. The person who walked out on you and forced you to face the birth of our child alone, because my work came first in those days.*

"Since we're taking a vacation together, I guess we must know each other fairly well."

Brett almost smiled at the speculative tone of her voice. Although he longed to tell her that they'd once shared a rare emotional and sensual closeness, he restrained himself. "We've known each other for several years, Leah. We met in D.C. when you were working as a congressional aide. I was stationed at the Pentagon."

"What are we?"

"To each other?" he asked quietly.

Leah nodded, her gaze sweeping across his sturdy-looking face for some clue about their relationship.

"I'd like to think we're friends."

She frowned. "Friends? We seem like more."

"We're just friends, Leah."

"Is that why you're taking care of me now?"

"You . . . we were headed up to the Pacific Northwest for a vacation," he said, modifying the truth somewhat. He knew this wasn't the time to tell her that he'd intended simply to follow her at a safe distance, stepping in only if she needed his help in defending herself against an unexpected attack. "We'd planned to end the trip by visiting your family in Seattle."

Leah sighed in obvious frustration and slumped

back against the sofa cushions. Brett released his hold on her hand the instant she started to tug free of him.

"I don't remember anything. Not a trip, not my name, not my life or my family, and not you. This is crazy."

"During my navy days I saw men with head wounds temporarily forget their entire lives, but they always got their memories back. You need to be patient."

"I don't feel patient," she grumbled. "I feel disconnected. Are we really friends? Or are you just doing a job of some kind?"

He met Leah's troubled gaze. Despite his desire to draw her into his arms and simply hold her, he kept himself under control and said, "You aren't a job, Leah. You never could be."

"You carry a gun. At first I thought I might be a criminal, or something equally awful."

He recalled her aversion to weapons of any kind, even though he and Micah had taken her target shooting when they'd all lived in the Washington, D.C., area. "I'm in federal law enforcement," he said, stretching the truth to accommodate the situation.

"It suits you somehow. The gun, I mean."

All the expression left his face. "Carpenters carry hammers," Brett said as he remembered the heated discussions they'd once had about gun control. "I carry a weapon, but I'll keep it out of sight if it bothers you."

"Oddly enough, it doesn't bother me, but it might under normal conditions. Whatever 'normal' is." She frowned again. "Are you going to take me back to Monterey now?"

"Is that what you want?" he asked in a level voice that he hoped concealed his concern that she might insist on returning home. Protecting her would be easier if they remained on the move.

"Not really. If you don't mind, I'd like to stick with our vacation plans. Then, if I don't remember anything by the time we get to Seattle, maybe seeing my family will jog my memory."

She absently trailed her fingertips across the top of his large hand and then up his forearm. He tensed, her light touch sending charged currents of heat into his flesh that made his muscles bunch beneath her fingertips.

"I don't want to be alone right now," she admitted in a small, vulnerable voice that made his heart ache.

"I don't intend to leave you alone, so don't worry."

She hesitantly met his piercing gaze. "Thank you."

"For what?" Brett asked as he got to his feet. He felt too tempted by his craving to reacquaint himself with the curves and hollows of her shapely body to remain in such close proximity to her. Hungry, too, for a lingering taste of her, he clenched his fists as he moved into the center of the room. His body, painfully aroused, fought him and briefly denied him the control he sought. Brett drew in a shuddery breath. And then another.

"For everything, but especially for being my friend."

Surprised by the obvious sincerity of her remark, he turned to look at her. He started to speak just as someone knocked on the door. His hand strayed to his gun. Brett stopped himself from reaching for it when he saw the startled look on Leah's face.

"Force of habit, I'm afraid," he said, trying to explain reflexes too ingrained to abandon. "Stay put."

Startled by his order, she laughed, "Yes, sir."

He grinned at her then, the change in his facial features provoking a stunning transformation. His dark eyes twinkled, his even white teeth flashed, and the upward curve of his lips seduced. Neither pretty nor handsome, Brett Upton personified the classic raw-boned, barely civilized male who rarely questioned his own prowess when dealing with the fairer sex or dangerous situations. None of the desire, self-doubt, or guilt he felt showed, but all those emotions and more thrived within his heart and mind.

"I liked the sound of that. Want to try it again?" he teased in spite of his inner turmoil.

Leah scowled at him, but amusement lingered in the depths of her blue-green eyes. "Don't hold your breath. It felt totally out of character."

Brett nodded, his expression growing unexpectedly pensive as he gave her a final probing look. "Trust me, it is."

As he walked to the sitting-room door, Brett resigned himself to the fury he knew she would feel once she regained her memory. Although he didn't want her amnesia to last too long, he savored her unguarded behavior and her willingness to depend on him.

Until she rejected him, he intended to watch over her with the vigilance of an avenging angel. No one, he silently vowed, would be permitted to harm her. No one.

Once the current threat ended and her life returned to normal, Brett planned to resume his role as distant protector, because he realized he had no right to expect anything more of Leah or of a child who didn't even know him. It was a role necessitated by his counterterrorism work, which he'd grudgingly accepted during the last six years, a role aided by Micah Holbrook, who administered the secret trust fund Brett had created for the woman he still loved and the little boy he'd fathered.

Three

Clad in an ankle-length, sapphire-silk nightgown, Leah lingered in front of the bathroom mirror and studied her reflection. She saw a tangled mane of golden hair that cascaded over slender shoulders and down a narrow back, large blue-green eyes rimmed by thick, dark-gold eyelashes, and a flawless complexion that looked as pale as ivory parchment paper. The smudges beneath her eyes emphasized the fatigued condition of her body, and the bump on her head still throbbed, but she felt fortunate that her earlier, mind-numbing pain had been replaced by a dull ache that no longer frightened her.

Frustrated by her lack of recognition and desperate to make some kind of contact with her real self, Leah searched her reflection. She stood very still. Hoping for a miracle, she waited. She hardly dared to breathe. Sighing finally, her shoulders slumped in defeat because she found nothing familiar in the face of the woman who peered back at her. Nor could she recall the fall she'd apparently taken earlier that night.

Who am I? she wondered as she bowed her head and pressed her fingertips to her aching temples. *Why can't I remember my life?*

Leah straightened and glanced once more at her reflection, but this time she studied the trim, high-breasted body that came with the fair complexion and waist-length hair. While she couldn't deny the perfect fit of the silk gown she'd found in the luggage Brett had carried into her bedroom, she felt as though she had dressed for bed in someone else's clothing. Too unsettled to continue her inspection of herself, she stepped away from the mirror and crossed the bathroom on bare feet.

Leah tugged open the door, but she hesitated in the doorway when she noticed Brett, who stood near the head of the bed that dominated the bedroom. They stared at each other for a long moment.

Despite her exhaustion and the late hour, Leah's senses responded to the unguarded hunger she saw in his eyes. She felt shaken right down to her toes by the quickening taking place deep inside her body, just as she felt almost fatalistic in her acceptance of Brett's ability to arouse her by simply looking at her with dark, penetrating eyes that spoke volumes about his skill as a lover.

She finally mustered the courage to cross the room. Leah watched Brett as she slowly approached him, never taking her eyes from the hard contours of his face as her heart performed a tap dance in her chest. Pausing just a few inches from him, she discovered that she didn't possess the strength or the will to end their eye contact.

She felt seared all over by the heat emanating from his gaze and his body. It seemed to encompass and then consume her until her knees felt weak and her pulse raced.

She reached out to him, but he deflected her hands before she could touch him. Stung by his rejection, she held very still. She suddenly realized that he knew just how close she was to surrendering to instincts that urged her to discard every ounce of common sense she possessed and simply go with the moment.

"Feel better?" he asked.

"Yes, much better. Having a shower helped me relax."

"You'll be able to sleep now."

Brett stepped past her. He jerked back the bedcovers and shoved aside all the pillows but one. Alarmed by his abrupt behavior, Leah placed her hand on his arm. He turned to look at her. The light from a nearby lamp cast shadows across his face and enhanced the tension etched into his hard features. She searched his expression with worried eyes, desperate to understand both his changed manner and his current state of mind.

"Leah . . ."

"Don't be angry with me. I'm not sure what I was thinking before. It's just that touching you feels . . . right."

"I'm not angry." He exhaled, air gusting out of his body before he muttered a harsh word that made Leah flinch. He then shoved the fingers of his free hand through his thick hair in a gesture of frustration. "I'm just worried about you. You didn't eat much, and you need to keep up your strength. Especially now."

"I guess I wasn't that hungry." *For anything but you,* she realized.

He nodded and moved around her, his hands clenched into fists at his sides. "Do you need anything else?"

She shook her head, but she instantly regretted the back-and-forth motion. "I'm fine."

"Get some rest, Leah. You'll feel better in the morning."

"Wait, please."

He paused. She sensed his reluctance to linger when he looked at her and then glanced away.

"I may not understand everything that's happening, but I trust you, Brett."

She didn't expect his stunned look. Before she could question him, he reached out and tugged her forward so that she stood beside the lamp. She didn't protest when he cupped her head in his hands and tilted her face upward. If anything, she liked the fact that he wanted to touch her.

Closing her eyes, Leah basked in the possessive feel of his hands. She swayed, her silk-covered lower body brushing against him. She felt him stiffen, but she also felt the hard ridge that revealed his desire for her.

"Look at me, Leah."

Already startled by the condition of his body and the charged currents arcing between them, she froze. Her eyes snapped open. She stared at him, too shocked by the answering arousal bursting to life inside her to protest his harsh-sounding order. Her thoughts and emotions confused, her gaze riveted on his face, she remained motionless as he inspected her eyes.

"How's your headache?" He lowered his hands and carefully worked the tight muscles at her nape. "Is the pain finally letting up?"

She felt her muscles start to unravel, just a second before her insides began to melt like candle wax placed atop a flame. She sighed, the sound as faint as butterfly wings brushing up against the petal of a flower.

"It's manageable now," she answered softly, her head falling backward and all the muscles in her body going slack. She peered up at him through half-lowered lashes, fascinated by the intensity she saw in his thickly lashed eyes and character-filled face and stunned by the potency of his body and his touch.

Leah welcomed the weight and strength of his big hands when he briefly placed them on her shoulders. As he slid them down the length of her arms, she had the impression that he was fighting some fierce inner battle. She also sensed that she was responsible for it. She fought her own battle, torn between the emotional chaos of not knowing her identity and the feelings Brett evoked.

"If you need anything, just call out."

"I will," she promised. "I honestly didn't mean to make you uncomfortable before. It's just that my emotions are really out of control right now. I'd like to think I'm not some clingy female who can't function without a man to lean on."

Brett looked strained, but he managed a tight smile. "You aren't some clingy female. You never have been, and you never could be. For the record, I'm not sorry you reached out to me, Leah, but you're vulnerable. Taking advantage of you isn't at the top of my list of things to do tonight. We're friends. I care enough about you to observe all the rules that go along with friendship."

Color spotted her cheeks. Embarrassed, she slipped free of him, climbed into bed, and drew the covers up to her chin. Leah pretended to be calm and in control, but her body continued to tremble, and she felt heat streaming through her veins like rivers of flame.

Brett turned off the bedside lamp. Leah caught his hand before he stepped away from the bed. She felt his gaze sweep over her like a brushfire, and she scrambled to remember the question she wanted to ask.

"Will you tell me about my life tomorrow?"

"I'll tell you everything you need to know, but only if you get some sleep."

She gave him a troubled look. "I can't remember the people in the photos I found in my wallet, but they're my family, aren't they?"

"Most of them," he conceded, his voice low and rough.

"Do you really think I'll get it all back?"

Brett released her hand and tucked it beneath the covers. "If I have anything to say about it, your life will be back to normal as quickly as possible."

"I don't know how to thank—"

He leaned down and kissed her forehead. "Then don't, because there's no need."

"Yes, there is," she whispered as she fought back tears and the urge to wrap her arms around his neck and just hold on. She raised her hand and gently stroked the side of his face. Her fingertips tingled, and her hand started to shake. "This would be a total nightmare if you weren't here to help me deal with it."

Still bent over her, he covered her hand and pressed it to his strong jaw. She felt the prickle of a beard that needed shaving, the warmth of his vital skin, and the tantalizing strength of his long, narrow fingers. She breathed in the faintly woodsy scent of his flesh, and then she exhaled shakily. A shudder rumbled through him. She heard the ragged sigh that followed, and she felt certain that they were, or had once been, more than friends. Much, much more.

Brett straightened, his spine rigid as he walked away from her. He hesitated near the door. "You aren't alone, and I have no intention of leaving you alone. I'll be with you every step of the way, Leah. That's a promise. Now, close your eyes and rest. I'll be in and out to check on you while you sleep."

Exhausted, Leah closed her eyes and sank back against the pillow. As she drifted into a restless doze, she questioned Brett's denial of the chemistry between them. She was attracted to him, and she felt certain that he desired her. Why, then, she wondered, did he feel inclined to deny the obvious?

I trust you.

Her words echoed in his head like a repetitive accusation. Brett laughed mirthlessly as he paced the sitting room. He knew he didn't deserve Leah's trust. He'd never deserved it.

He couldn't relax, and he didn't even try to sleep. When he wasn't pacing in an effort to control the fever in his blood and relieve the heaviness in his loins, he periodically checked on Leah in the hours that followed. He hated waking her, but he grasped the necessity of making sure that she hadn't relapsed into the semiconscious state of the evening before.

Brett castigated himself for placing her in jeopardy when he wasn't planning the route they would take into the Pacific Northwest once she was rested enough to travel. He also struggled, on a minute-by-minute basis, against remembering the passion and love they'd once shared, but he failed to discard the memories that haunted him.

He still craved her tenderness. He knew he always would, especially in the face of his escalating dissatisfaction with the cold, violence-filled world he'd inhabited for the last several years.

Dressed in a pair of snug, partially fastened jeans and nothing more, Brett slipped into Leah's bedroom shortly before dawn. Aware that the first twenty-four hours following a head injury were the most crucial, he knew he had to disturb her yet again. After switching on the bedside lamp, he sat down on the edge of the bed. He reached for her as he reminded himself that her memory could return at any moment.

Leah opened her eyes. Brett saw the clarity and focus of her gaze, and he realized that she was wide awake. "You should be asleep."

She smiled and stretched. As she raised her arms, her breasts swelled above the lace bodice of her nightgown. Brett closed the hands he wanted to fill with her silky flesh into fists and dragged his eyes up to her heart-shaped face.

"So should you," she countered as she lowered her arms. "What's wrong?"

He cleared his throat twice before he answered her. "Nothing. I just wanted to make sure you're all right."

"Were you a doctor in another life?" Her smile widened as she pulled herself up against the headboard of the bed. "Or maybe a compulsive mother hen?"

He chuckled, his tension lessened by her humor. "Not that I know of, but I've had extensive first-aid training courtesy of the navy."

"I'm fine. Really. I've just got a lot of thoughts racing around in my head, so I keep waking up."

"What kind of thoughts?" he asked with quiet concern.

"Nothing in particular. Definitely nothing to worry about, so you can stop scowling at me." She smoothed her fingertips across the top of his clenched fist until he opened his hand and let her lace their fingers together. "I'm glad you're here."

"Me too. How's your headache?"

"Not too bad." She gave him a conspiratorial grin. "Why are we whispering?"

"Probably because most of the world's still asleep."

"Brett Matthew Upton."

"That's me." He silently applauded her memory of their earlier conversation.

"I like the sound of your name. It's sturdy and reliable, like you."

Brett knew the truth. She hadn't been able to rely on him when she'd needed him most. He'd failed her, and he didn't expect ever to be able to undo the damage of his actions.

She looked away from his intent gaze. "I've been dreaming about you."

"Why?" His voice was hoarse. He was almost afraid to hear her answer.

"I'm not sure."

"Any nightmares?"

"None that I recall."

He said a silent thank-you for that small favor. Brett hated the possibility that she might be haunted by nightmares of the men who'd tried to kidnap her.

She dropped her eyes to their laced fingers. After studying them for several silent seconds, she whispered, "Will you hold me for a little while?"

"Now?" Motionless as he sat there, he worked at concealing both his surprise at her request and his hunger for any contact that she felt inclined to allow.

Leah nodded. "You make me feel safe." She lifted her face, the worry he saw in her eyes revealing the true depth of her vulnerability. "I need to feel safe."

Brett nodded, got up, and walked around the bed, his thoughts in disarray as he joined her. Despite his concern that he was tempting fate, he stretched out atop the bedspread, jammed a few pillows behind his back before settling against the headboard, and then drew Leah into his arms.

When she turned into him and rested her head against his bare shoulder, he felt his heart stutter to a lengthy stop. It eventually began to beat again, but at a hectic pace when he felt her slender fingers sink into the thick mat of dark hair that covered his chest and belly. He responded instantly to her closeness and to her touch, his nerve endings igniting, his muscles tensing beneath her fingertips, and his sex straining beneath the increasingly snug fit of his jeans.

"Are we lovers, Brett?"

He felt shock pummel his senses like a fighter gone mad in the ring.

Shifting in his arms, she peered up at him. "Are we?" she asked once more.

He exhaled shakily. "No, Leah, we aren't lovers." *We haven't been for a long time, but it isn't because I don't want you every second of every day.*

"Then why do I feel as though we've been intimate? Why else would I feel so comfortable one minute and so aroused the next?" She moved out of his arms to kneel on the bed near his hips. "Why would I trust you so completely? Why do I want to make love with you every time you look at me or touch me? Why would I want you now if we aren't lovers?" she asked, her voice rising in pitch with each question.

He seized her by the waist, dragged her into his lap, and held her despite her initial struggle. Although still grappling with her unexpected candor, he spoke calmly. "I'm glad you trust me." Brett thought of all the reasons why she shouldn't. The list was as long as his arm. "But I can't tell you why you feel that we've been intimate."

"I'm making a fool of myself, throwing myself at you this way. You must think I'm some kind of raving idiot." She rested her forehead against his chin and sighed.

He wrapped his arms around her, the sound of her frustrated sigh and the tension he felt in her slender limbs making him hate himself. "I don't think you're anything of the kind. You've been through a lot during the last twelve hours, so relax and give yourself a break, why don't you?"

She squirmed free of him, eased backward, and wound up astride the aching ridge of flesh that proclaimed his maleness. Brett shifted beneath her, but he couldn't hide the reality she'd discovered.

"You want me too," she accused. "I can feel how much you want me." She lowered her hand to a spot just above the half-open zipper of his jeans. She paused, drew in a shaky breath, and then trailed her fingers through the coarse thatch of dark hair at the base of his abdomen, her gaze fixed on his strained features the entire time. He jerked beneath her gliding fingertips. "You . . . want . . . me."

The muscles bunched in his jaw as he ground his teeth together. After slowly counting to ten, he spoke. "I'm not going to deny the obvious, but this isn't the time or the place, Leah." He pushed her hand aside when all he really wanted to do was flip her onto her back and plunge into her body.

"That was stupid of me," she admitted.

"I'm trying to make allowances for you tonight, but pull another stunt like that again and all bets are off."

She absently rubbed her wrist. "You seemed surprised earlier when I told you I trusted you. Why?"

"I'm no Boy Scout."

"And I'm too old to be a Girl Scout. So where does that leave us?" she challenged, a reckless glint in her eyes.

This wasn't the Leah he remembered, Brett realized. Micah had warned him that she'd grown assertive and outspoken, but he hadn't listened. He knew now that he should have.

He tugged her forward so that she rested against the hard wall of his chest. He methodically stroked her back until he felt her breathing slow to an even pace. When she sighed, he felt the wash of her warm breath against his neck and knew she'd finally stopped fighting herself and him.

"Talk to me, please," Leah whispered. "Tell me about my life. I need to know about myself."

"Your thirtieth birthday was last month," he began, his voice steady despite the physical stress of having her molded against his body. "You're beautiful and funny and smart. People have always liked you. You're one of the most honest women I've ever known, and you aren't afraid to get your hands dirty if there's work to be done. You're strong and courageous in a crisis, and you're compassionate when your friends need you."

Surprise and pleasure brightened her eyes as she eased back and stared at him. "I sound like a nice person."

"You're more than nice. Much more," he said, his voice low and his eyes so dark that they looked black.

She sank against him once more, her breasts plumping against his hard chest, her gently rounded stomach mating with the rock-solid surface of his belly, and her soft inner thighs bracketing his narrow hips and hard loins. Wrapping her arms around him, she rested her head on his shoulder and closed her eyes.

Brett continued to run his hands up and down her narrow back. He lost track of time and the world. Focused on Leah, he felt every breath she took and heard every sigh that escaped her. She began to drift off, her shapely body going slack against him. He felt as though someone had poured hot honey over his tense body.

Lowering his hands once he heard the measured cadence of her deepening respiration, he cupped her silk-swathed hips, closed his eyes, and savored his sensual memories of the woman in his arms. The woman whose skin turned to hot satin in the throes of passion, the woman who'd always given of herself with sensual generosity and spontaneity, and the woman who had conceived a son in his bed before he'd thrown her away like a fool.

As his mind continued to produce a series of erotic images, Brett's body tightened until he felt that so much as a glance from Leah would incinerate his soul. He inhaled, taking in the scent of her skin, and then he exhaled raggedly. He shuddered a few seconds later, aware that he couldn't risk having her in his arms much longer. Moving carefully, he shifted her off his lap and back onto the bed.

"What's the matter?" she asked as he settled her

on her pillow and smoothed her hair away from her face.

"Nothing. Go back to sleep," he urged, his palm resting against her cheek as he leaned over her.

Her eyes fluttered closed. She turned her face to his open palm and pressed her lips to his callused skin, shocking him with the wet glide of the tip of her tongue and the imprint of her lips.

She branded him and humbled him in that instant. Even without a single memory of her life, he realized that Leah still possessed the instinct-driven ability to express her feelings.

The dam restraining his emotions and desires crumbled under the force of her tender kiss. Desperate for the taste of her, he relinquished the control he'd always demanded of himself and took her mouth. Shattering hunger and painful arousal dominated him. Brett abandoned his private war of resistance and reclaimed what had been his so long ago, his lips and tongue seeking and finding the sweet, hot passion that only Leah could give him.

Her lips parted almost instantly. Her tongue darted into his mouth. She tasted like the finest wine. He felt her hands as she gripped his shoulders. Her nails scored his flesh, but he experienced nothing resembling pain. A heartbeat later he registered the restless movement of her legs as she kicked free of the covers and molded her body to his. He didn't know where she stopped and he began, and he didn't care.

He'd lost his mind, he realized. There was only now and Leah and his need, the latter a steady, consuming force streaming through his veins with blazing intent.

He felt consumed as she answered each thrust of his tongue. He felt whole because her arms were around him and she was clinging to him and moaning his name. He felt loved for the first time in years. And then he felt like the worst kind of bastard on the planet, because she was vulnerable and he was on the verge of taking advantage of her. He knew in his heart that he didn't deserve her.

She wouldn't want you if she remembered you, his conscience reminded him. *She'd reject you, just as you rejected her.*

Brett tore his mouth from hers. Leah groaned in protest, reaching out to him, blindly trying to reestablish contact, but he held her away from him, his head thrown back, his eyes squeezed shut, and his body in agony as he tried to reclaim his sanity.

He rolled away from her once he found the strength to move. When he finally met her stunned gaze, he saw the rosy blush of passion that flushed her cheeks and the dazed look in her eyes that spoke of her bewilderment. Cursing himself, he jerked upright and sat on the edge of the bed, his hands covering his face as air gusted in and out of a body that shook and screamed with need.

He felt her fingertips glide down his spine, her touch tentative, uncertain. He flinched when she spoke his name. Brett knew if he glanced at her now, he'd find concern, not recrimination in her expressive features.

He forced himself to his feet. He straightened slowly, trembling as he turned to look down at her. Propped up on one arm, she stared at him. His gaze fell to her silk-draped body, and he saw the swift rise and fall of her full, hard-nippled breasts. He thought of the pregnancy she'd faced alone and the tiny infant she'd nursed, and he felt a new wave of self-loathing sweep across him.

"I'm sorry," he managed in a voice that sounded

like gears grinding. He headed for the bedroom door, moving swiftly but without his usual predatory grace.

"I'm not sorry, Brett," she declared. "I'm not sorry at all. We're adults, not children. Denying the obvious seems pretty stupid to me. Even though I don't understand what's going on between us, I still trust you and feel safe with you. That's not going to change. I hope you'll decide to explain why you're fighting the feelings we apparently share." She paused briefly, a thoughtful expression on her face. "You weren't wearing a wedding ring, but that doesn't mean anything one way or the other in this day and age, does it?"

Still gripping the doorknob, he half turned to look at her. "I'm not married, Leah. Neither are you."

"That's encouraging," she said dryly. "You care about me, don't you, even though you don't want to."

"Yes, I care about you, but we aren't lovers. I was telling you the truth."

She sank back against a plump pillow. For a moment she busied herself with the task of arranging the covers over her slender body. After smoothing them into place with shaking fingers, she looked at him and gently said, "Perhaps we should be."

"No, Leah, we shouldn't be. You deserve better than me." Brett walked out of the room, slamming the door behind him and cursing his self-indulgent behavior.

Four

Leah felt a profound sense of abandonment settle over her the instant Brett slammed out of the room. Stunned by the depth of the emotional isolation his departure caused, she rolled onto her side, curled into herself, and closed her eyes.

The dull throbbing of her head eased somewhat as she slowly inhaled and exhaled to calm herself, but her measured breathing did little to assuage either the tension humming through her or the desire that made her body ache for completion. She still tasted Brett on her lips, and the scent of his skin lingered in her senses. Recalling the tempered power of his embrace, Leah trembled anew.

She focused on clearing her thoughts and reclaiming her equilibrium, but she discovered that Brett was permanently etched into her sensory memory. Bewildered by his denial of their obvious mutual attraction, she began to suspect that he didn't trust himself with her. She couldn't help wondering why.

Although she lacked the safety net of actually knowing how she'd spent the previous thirty years of her life, Leah felt oddly reassured by the rainbow of emotions Brett aroused in her. She also felt curious about and compelled to explore each and every emotion, primarily because of the sense of completeness she'd found in his arms as the recipient of his passion. Remembering, too, how he'd wrenched free of her, she felt both a need to understand what had happened between them and a renewed sense of emptiness.

She whispered a quiet prayer that she would eventually remember all the facets of her relationship with Brett once she accessed the dark void that held her memories. Despite his insistence, Leah felt certain now that they weren't *just friends*. She believed, instead, that they shared a history worthy of her scrutiny.

Had he hurt her? Leah wondered. Had she failed to absolve him of the guilt he felt? Had *she* wounded him, perhaps even rejected him? She couldn't imagine doing such a stupid thing, but she supposed that almost anything was possible. Was he reluctant to forgive her? Was he standing by her now because he wanted to or simply because he felt obligated? Was she some fickle creature who used and discarded men?

Her final thought bothered her the most. She didn't want to think of herself as cruel or heartless, but she refused to ignore the possibility or to cast herself in a positive light simply because she had no memory of herself. She speculated that what she considered Brett's reticence might actually be a volatile mix of caution and desire on his part.

Despite the unexpected nature of her feelings for Brett, and even though she worried that she might be reaching out to him because he represented stability in the face of chaos, she desired him in every way a woman desires a man. Leah sighed as she looked beyond the dim glow of the bedside lamp to the sheer drapes that covered the window across the room.

Dawn had crept into the sky since Brett's exit from her bedroom. She felt her frustration grow as she struggled with questions that had no answers. Answers, at least, that were beyond her grasp as things stood now. Although she didn't understand why, she sensed that Brett Upton occupied a crucial position in her life.

She couldn't deny that his darkly erotic nature intrigued and seduced her. His touch aroused her to an incendiary state. Leah hesitated once again, wondering if she was guilty of embroidering reality or if she should take a chance and trust instincts that prompted her to conclude that she'd experienced a kaleidoscope of feelings and emotions with him in the past.

Leah pondered his actions and reactions in the hours they'd spent together. She sensed a vulnerability in Brett that he tried to hide behind a rough, aggressive exterior. Having experienced his gentle concern and having viewed the worry etched into his rugged features when he thought she wasn't watching him, she knew better than to ever think that he was a cold or careless man. She'd felt the infernolike heat of his embrace and the strength of his desire. He cared about her. As a woman, not just as a friend. She knew it in her heart, even though he seemed determined to maintain a platonic relationship.

Too restless to sleep, Leah muttered an unladylike word and sat up. She spotted her purse on the bedside table. Reaching for the leather shoulder bag, she drew it into her lap and extracted her wallet. She poked through the contents once more, desperate for a place to start in her effort to rebuild her life and hopeful that she might trigger even the most inconsequential of memories.

After turning up the wattage of the bedside lamp, she lingered over the photographs in the wallet. A group photo of more than a dozen people taken on the front steps of a church following a wedding service—a smiling Leah stood beside the bride—hinted that she might be part of a large, loving family that looked like a recruiting poster for Viking men and their petite, golden-haired women.

Brett, who stood at the edge of the gathering, was the only dark-haired man in the group. A second photo, this one of herself and several children seated atop a picnic table in what appeared to be a densely wooded park, made her pause.

All the children except one were grinning, slim-limbed sprites with golden hair, fair skin, and possibly the offspring, she decided, of some of the adults in the first photograph. The exception, a serious-looking little boy of about four or five, was dark-eyed, raven-haired, and sturdily built.

Leah's gaze lingered on the young boy. His darker features served to set him apart from the other children. She gripped the photo, instinct more than anything else prompting her to study his image closely. A pinpoint of light flickered in the recesses of her mind, a teasing flicker of recognition that died unexpectedly as she peered at the child's face. She sensed something familiar about him, but she failed to connect him to a specific past memory as she sat there and concentrated.

She reluctantly moved on to a third photograph, a posed shot of a mature couple in their late fifties. Leah saw herself in the delicate-featured woman whose hair had turned white and whose eyes were a pale blue-green version of her own. She felt a moment of panic as she studied a picture of the two people who had probably given her life, raised her, and cared for her until she'd set out into the world on her own.

She felt her panic give way to fear. Fear that she might never remember the people who loved her. Fear that produced tears she couldn't stop and sobs that shook her slender body as she sank back against the pillows. Clutching the photographs, she wept for everything and everyone she couldn't remember. She also wept for herself, although she knew self-pity wouldn't solve the crisis of not knowing her identity.

Leah fell asleep as her sobs abated. The image of the small, dark-haired boy stayed with her as her breathing slowed and deepened. She took him into her dreams, and she found comfort in his presence there. When she wakened several hours later, Leah discovered that she still held all three photographs.

After a few hours of much-needed rest, Brett telephoned Micah Holbrook from the privacy of his bedroom. He confirmed that a kidnapping attempt had been made against Leah, but he assured his old friend that his younger sister was safe and would remain that way.

With Micah's sardonically voiced best wishes ringing in his ears, Brett also learned of the preliminary success of Interpol, in conjunction with a Naval Intelligence team headed by Micah, in arresting several known members of the terrorist faction the two men had pursued for the last several years. The leader and his top lieutenants, according to Micah, were still at large, but within their grasp.

Brett then placed a second call to the individual responsible for the protection of his son and Leah's parents, who were tucked away in a remote fishing cabin in southwestern Canada with a contingent of security guards. He issued an order that the three were to remain in seclusion until the last of the terrorists were taken into custody. He also requested that a physician join the group, because he shared Micah's worry about the senior Holbrook's heart condition.

Relieved by the encouraging update and aware that he was free to concentrate fully on Leah's well-being, Brett quickly showered, shaved, and dressed. He heard her moving around in her bedroom and private bath as he walked into the sitting room. Pleased that she was awake, he ordered a full brunch for two and additional coffee.

Brett poured himself a cup of coffee from a half-empty carafe that he'd ordered earlier and drank it while he browsed the editorial page of a local San Francisco newspaper. He glanced up a little while later when Leah opened her bedroom door and stepped into the sitting room. Clad in a pair of form-fitting jeans, a long-sleeved, pale-pink knit top, and a pair of athletic shoes, she looked refreshed and relaxed.

"I smell coffee," she said by way of a greeting.

"There's plenty." He gestured in the direction of a coffee service positioned in the center of the low, teak table in front of the couch. "Help yourself. Room service should be here in a few minutes."

She smiled as she poured a cup. "I have a craving for eggs Benedict."

Brett recalled the lazy weekends, long hours of lovemaking, and leisurely morning-after brunches they'd shared at a bed-and-breakfast inn on the

Virginia coast. He remembered, too, how the world had ceased to matter during those interludes of passion and serenity.

"You always crave eggs Benedict when you sleep late," he told her. "I'm glad your appetite's back. That's a good sign."

"It's returned in a big way," she confirmed as she sat down on the couch. "I'm starved."

"You look rested this morning."

She nodded before taking a sip of her coffee. "I feel better." She grimaced as her taste buds embraced and then recoiled from the strong brew.

"You hate black coffee."

"You're right."

"You use honey, whenever it's available. You've never used cream."

"Thanks," she said as she leaned forward and reached for the natural sweetener. Leah glanced his way after stirring two heaping teaspoons of honey into the steaming black liquid. "It's kind of strange to realize that you know more about me than I do."

"I pay attention to the details," he admitted quietly as he revitalized his senses with the sight of her delicate beauty and the white-ginger scent of her skin. He felt his body respond, as it invariably did, to her nearness.

"Given your profession, I guess that's not surprising."

His desire eased, but didn't completely depart. Brett gave her a thoughtful look, but he didn't press her for an explanation of her remark. Leah, he knew, liked to conduct verbal fishing expeditions, but he felt prepared to handle her curiosity. "Any residual pain?"

"The brass band is gone, if that's what you're asking."

"I'm asking for a more complete statement, Leah."

"I have a very mild headache. I doubt it'll last much longer, so you can stop worrying now."

He folded the newspaper and dropped it on the floor beside his chair. "Friends worry about friends."

Her smile faded. "Is that really what we are?"

"I hope so."

Leah looked away. He watched her concentrate on her coffee. He noticed that she flinched and her fingers strayed to her temple when a series of sharp knocks sounded on the door a few minutes later.

"Finish your coffee," he ordered brusquely. "I'll answer it."

Brett got to his feet and crossed the room, moving with the fluidity and stealth of a man accustomed to confronting and disposing of any threat he encountered. Alert to everything around him, he registered Leah's silence as he greeted the room-service waiter at the door. He signed the check, thanked the young man, and then took control of a cart that held several covered dishes, a cloth-covered basket of muffins, and another carafe of coffee. After closing and locking the door, he wheeled the cart into the room and parked it beside a small table.

"Eggs Benedict for two, a double side order of hash browns, fresh-squeezed orange juice, extra muffins, and another pot of coffee."

Startled by her precise recitation of the room-service order he'd placed before she'd joined him in the sitting room, Brett stiffened for a moment before turning to look at her. "Where did that come from?"

"Somewhere out in left field, I suppose." She got up from the sofa, approached him, and helped him transfer the contents of the cart to the table.

"Do you . . ." he began, a mixture of hope and dread filtering into his heart.

"I don't remember anything." She sat down and accepted the linen napkin Brett handed her. After surveying the meal he'd ordered, Leah remarked, "Spooky, isn't it?"

He joined her at the table, unfolded his napkin, and placed it in his lap. "I'd call it encouraging."

"Perhaps," she conceded as she ran her fingertip across the backs of the photos she'd placed face-down on the table beside her plate. "Even though I didn't recognize anything in my suitcases, I felt like I knew what I was looking for as I got dressed this morning."

He reached out and took her free hand, his need to reassure her intensifying the darkness of his gaze and tightening his jaw. He saw her surprise in the widening of her eyes and in the flush that tinted her skin. When he felt the faint tremors that shook her fingers, he sensed that she, too, remembered the heated moments they'd shared just before the dawn.

Consciously sidestepping the riot of emotions he felt, Brett observed, "Your instincts are taking over. That's the first step, Leah. Don't fight the process. Just let yourself roll with it."

She withdrew her hand from his grasp and picked up her knife and fork. "I'm trying."

He watched her, his gaze steady. Tension rose up inside him when she suddenly let her silverware fall from her fingers. Leah sank back in her chair, her expressive features troubled.

"Talk to me," he urged.

She studied him for a long moment. "You're very protective of me. When someone knocks on the door, you tell me to stay put. Last night I thought it was funny, but now I get the oddest feeling that you're trying to shield me from something or someone. Why?"

"I care about you. If our positions were reversed, I'd like to think you'd feel protective of me."

"As a friend?"

He heard the edge in her voice, not just her disbelief. "As a friend," he agreed calmly. "Let's declare a truce, why don't we? I'm not the enemy."

"Is friendship all you want from me?"

"That's an unfair question right now."

"I don't think it is, but I can't force you to say things you don't want to say. Fair warning, though, because I intend to ask that particular question again." Sighing in obvious frustration, she straightened in her chair and reached for a blueberry muffin from the basket in the center of the table. "I apologize for trying to back you into a corner. The stress of not remembering anything about our relationship or my life must be getting to me. I probably sound suspicious and paranoid. I don't mean to."

"Apology accepted." Acutely aware that she had every right in the world to be suspicious of him, Brett picked up the carafe and refilled both their coffee cups.

As if by mutual agreement, they concentrated on their food. Brett silently applauded Leah's enthusiastic consumption of her meal as he grew relaxed enough to enjoy the companionable calm they shared while they ate.

"Perfection," she announced twenty minutes later. After blotting her lips with her napkin, she poured herself a cup of coffee. "Absolute perfection. Do I always eat like this?"

Brett smiled. For such a petite woman, Leah had the appetite of a person three times her size. "For as long as I've known you." He reached for the last muffin in the basket.

Leah met his gaze, curiosity lighting her eyes. "And how long is that?"

"About eight years. Your brother introduced us."

"My brother?"

"Micah Holbrook."

"One of the Vikings?" she asked, her tone speculative.

His smile lingered, although he felt a jolt of surprise that she'd vocalized the code name Micah used when sending classified message traffic to the Pentagon brass. "That's a pretty good description of Micah, Jake, and Gavin, as well as your dad."

She grinned. "I have three brothers?"

He smiled back at her when he saw her delight. "And two sisters. Carrie and Diana. Micah's the oldest of the Holbrook tribe, and you're fourth in line."

She extracted one of the pictures from the stack beside her plate and handed it to Brett. "When did this wedding take place?"

When we were still together, he remembered, his smile fading as he glanced at the photo. When we were happy. When we were planning our own wedding.

"Quite a while ago. Diana, the bride, has five-year-old twin boys now. You and Carrie were her bridesmaids. Your brothers were ushers." He returned the photograph to her, aware of how precious family memorabilia of any kind was to her.

"You're wearing a tux in the picture, so I assume you were in the wedding party too."

"That's right. Your parents always made me feel like part of the family."

She took a second photograph and handed it to Brett. Their fingertips brushed. Leah inhaled sharply, her gaze shifting to Brett's face. He peered back at her, pretending he hadn't felt the hot spark that had passed between them.

"Are these people my parents?"

Her question had a breathless quality to it. Brett recalled how similar it was to the sound of her voice when they'd made love. He ached just thinking about what it would be like to hear her whispered words of pleasure as their bodies merged and she wrapped her arms and legs around him. His hand shook as he returned the photograph to Leah. She studied their faces, preoccupied enough, Brett hoped, not to notice that his fantasies about her were on the verge of disabling him.

"Helene and Martin Holbrook," he confirmed.

"Are they as nice as they look?"

"Even nicer. They love each other, and they adore their children. They've always reminded me of two sides of the same coin. Unique individuals, but permanently mated."

"I look like my mother, don't I?"

"All the girls in the family resemble Helene." Brett grinned. "But she's very even-tempered."

"And I'm not?" she asked, bristling a little.

"No, you're not. You tend to be self-contained until you're pushed too hard. Then you go off like a firecracker on the Fourth of July."

"How lovely," she muttered.

"It doesn't happen that often," Brett said with a chuckle. "What do you think of yourself so far?"

"I don't know what to think."

Leaning forward, he rested his forearms on the edge of the table. "Shall I tell you what I think of you?" he asked, aware that he tempted fate by even asking such a question.

Leah hesitated, but her curiosity showed, especially to a man who knew her well. She finally nodded. "Please."

"I think you're one of the most unique women I've ever known. You're sensitive and loving and fiercely loyal. You may have a temper, but it never gets out of control. I doubt that you've ever intentionally hurt anyone in your entire life."

"No one's that perfect. I'm sure I'm just as flawed as the next person, especially if I have the temper you just described."

He shrugged and accepted her final offering, the photo of the children gathered around her as they all sat atop a picnic table. He concealed his reaction to the picture by saying, "This must be from the Yellowstone camping trip." His attention riveted on the face of his small son, Brett stared at the picture for several minutes before he found the strength to refocus on Leah. As he spoke, he thought of how much he was missing of his son's life. "This was taken last summer at the official Holbrook family reunion. Everyone except Micah"— *and yours truly*, he recalled silently— "managed to attend."

"The children. Do I know them?" she asked.

Yellow caution flags waved in his mind. "Of course. There are a few strays in the group, but most of them are Holbrook grandchildren," he confirmed.

She looked at them, both frustration and hope in her expression. "They look like wonderful kids. When I studied this particular photo earlier, I thought I recognized one of them."

"What about now?" he asked, careful not to betray his emotions. He wasn't ready to talk about their son, and he knew it would serve no purpose other than to cause Leah additional anxiety.

She shook her head. "Not a single memory. Just

the nagging feeling that I should know them, especially the little boy with the dark hair and eyes."

Brett felt his heart stop beating for a moment. "It won't be long before you're able to put names to the faces, so don't torture yourself."

"I'll figure it out eventually," she vowed as she tucked the three photographs into the breast pocket of her knit top and reclaimed her coffee cup. "What do I do?"

Relieved to be off the subject of children, Brett readily answered her question. "You're the co-owner of a flower shop in Monterey, you do volunteer work with the homeless, and you own a Victorian home that you've spent the last four years restoring."

She looked startled. "All that? When do I sleep?"

He chuckled. "I've often asked myself the same question. You've always had more energy than any ten people I know."

"Is my flower shop successful? Who's my partner?"

"Very successful. Sarah Kelly's your partner. She was your roommate at college. She's a widow. No kids. You two have made quite a success of the business. You have contracts with some of the major hotels in Monterey, in addition to the normal business any flower shop does."

Brett spoke with the ease of a man who'd devoured and memorized every detail about the life of the woman he loved. Thanks to Micah, who understood better than anyone the risks involved in covert work for Naval Intelligence, and because Micah had always enjoyed a very close relationship with his younger sister, Brett read every letter she wrote to her brother, saw every photograph and home movie taken of her child, and heard the tapes of the weekly conversation the two siblings routinely shared whenever Micah was stateside.

Brett knew that Micah's loyalty was primarily to Leah and her child. Despite the temporary rift caused between the two men when Leah discovered her pregnancy, Micah accepted Brett's reasoning for remaining apart from her. He also shared Brett's desire to protect her. As a result, Micah became the conduit that allowed Brett to know his son and to assure Leah's safety.

"Is there a man in my life?"

"No, there isn't."

"I wonder why." She pinned him with a probing stare. "Do you know why?"

He shifted in his chair, trying to find a way to answer her. He knew better than to say, *I hurt you when I walked out on you. You haven't trusted anyone with your emotions since then. Part of me's glad, because maybe I'll get another chance with you, but another part of me's sad that you've had to face so much on your own.*

"Do you, Brett?"

"That's not a question I can answer. You've never said why you don't date, and I've never asked because I felt I'd be intruding on your privacy." He paused for a moment, carefully considering his next comment. "You're very independent, Leah. You always have been. You also have a lot of responsibilities. I can only assume that you've chosen not to complicate your life with a personal relationship."

"Perhaps it's something simpler. Maybe I got burned and decided to swear off the opposite sex altogether," she speculated.

"Maybe," he conceded, his voice tighter than an overwound spring and his expression closed.

Leah frowned. "Your voice is flat, and you look

kind of gray. Are you ill? Did I say something wrong?"

He mustered a tense smile. "No. You haven't done or said anything wrong."

She suddenly went very still, an expression of disbelief on her face. Her tone gentle and nonjudgmental, she asked, "Are you gay?"

Brett laughed, amazed by her question. "No, I'm not gay."

"I'm glad. Do you like me?"

He suspected that she actually meant, *Do you want me the way a man wants a woman?* "Very much."

"You said we aren't lovers. Were we at some point in the past?"

He groaned silently, because her curiosity was justified and he loathed lying to her. "Leah, that's not an experience a man would forget, especially with you. You're a beautiful and desirable woman."

She jumped to her feet, declaring in the process, "Well, I'm obviously a very frustrated one too! I feel like I'm on fire when you touch me. Just being knee-to-knee at this table makes me want you. You keep telling me we're just friends, but I'm having a hard time believing you." She stopped her pacing as abruptly as she'd begun it and whirled to face him. "Do you think becoming sexually overwrought is a result of getting bonked on the head? Do you suppose I'll feel like attacking every man I trip over until I get my memory back?"

In the process of taking a sip of coffee, Brett swallowed wrong and choked. He grabbed his napkin, blotting his mouth as he struggled to keep from roaring with laughter. His humor burst free in spite of his effort to contain it.

"This isn't funny!" she exclaimed. "There's obviously something very wrong with me, aside from my headache and bruises that make me look as though I have a second job as a punching bag."

Concerned about how agitated she was becoming, Brett frowned as she returned to her chair and sank down onto it. He leaned forward and covered the hand she placed atop the table with his own. "Relax. Your headache's sure to get worse if you don't settle down."

She shot him a baleful look, but she followed his suggestion and took deep, calming breaths. Brett gently stroked the back of her hand before lacing their fingers together. Smiling at her a few minutes later, he asked, "Better now?"

Leah nodded. "I like it when you touch me. I like it a lot."

He didn't miss her belligerent tone of voice. He savored her words, even though he knew she would never have spoken them under normal circumstances. The expression on her face informed him that she was waiting for him to contradict her. He didn't. He knew he never would.

"For the record, Leah, there's not a damn thing wrong with you that a little rest and relaxation won't cure. As for the chemistry between us, it's always been there."

"Then I'm not crazy."

"No crazier than I am, because I've always felt the pull between us," he admitted, glad for a chance to speak the truth.

"Shouldn't we do something about it?" she whispered.

He shook his head, his denial of the need he'd felt for so many years automatic. "Your job right now is to reclaim your life. My job is to help you. There's no time or space for anything else, Leah. If you're honest with yourself," Brett said, "you'll admit that I'm right." He clasped her hand more securely when she tried to draw from him. "We both know you're reaching out to me for the wrong reason. If you want me when you have your identity back, them I'm yours, but not until then. Once I take you into my bed and we make love, I don't want to be remembered as a mistake in judgment. That happened to me once, a long time ago. I can't let it happen again."

Looking stricken, Leah nodded, eased free of his grasp, and got up from her chair. Brett watched her slowly walk to the bedroom door, pause, and then glance over her shoulder. After staring at him for a long moment, Leah disappeared from sight.

Brett remained at the table, the food in his stomach turning to lumps of stone and the sound of Leah's bedroom door being closed echoing in his head. Once again, he felt shut out of her life. He loathed the familiar feeling.

Five

Leah retreated to the privacy of her bedroom, her thoughts and emotions in turmoil. She spent much of her time searching the dark corners of her mind for her past, studying the photographs she'd found in her wallet, and reflecting on her strong attraction to Brett.

Unable to sit still, she alternated between long hours of pacing and short naps, but she found neither comfort nor answers in either endeavor. Leah remained in her bedroom for the rest of the day, throughout the night, and well into the next day, emerging only once to share a silent evening meal with Brett in the sitting room.

She grappled simultaneously with the desire he inspired in her and with the anxiety created by her memory loss. Even though she sensed his comprehension of the true depth of the emotional confusion she felt, his patience with her self-imposed isolation still surprised her.

Grateful that Brett didn't demand an explanation of her behavior during their meal or when he periodically checked on her, Leah concentrated on finding the strength to accept the reality that she might have to face the future without ever regaining any knowledge of her past. She knew that people the world over faced greater tragedies on a daily basis, but that knowledge didn't lessen her fear. Praying that she wasn't deluding herself, she repeatedly told herself that she possessed the ability to confront the unknown.

Her desire for Brett refused to remain at bay. If anything, Leah realized, it escalated with each passing hour. It haunted her, too, because she knew he desired her in return.

She simultaneously appreciated and resented his restraint. He was, she realized almost grudgingly, a man of conscience. A man who refused to use a woman simply to slake his own physical hunger. A man honest enough to admit that he didn't want to be used either. She instinctively doubted that she'd ever known anyone quite like him.

Even though Brett moved through the rooms of the suite with usual predatory silence, Leah always felt his presence. He became the one constant in the sea of her unease. She began to count on his regular forays into her room, although few words passed between them.

She found courage in his quiet strength, despite the worry she glimpsed in his dark eyes when he watched her. Leah silently applauded him for not making her feel as though she needed to apologize for requiring a healthy chunk of time for herself. He wasn't, she concluded with both surprise and pleasure, the kind of man who judged or faulted the frailties of others.

Leah slept restlessly, when she slept at all, her dreams filled with faceless men who spoke a language she didn't understand. Alternately drenched in perspiration or chilled to the bone, she awoke often. Each time she escaped the torment of sleep, she found Brett watching over her, felt his hands skimming up and down her arms as he tried to soothe her. She tried several times to apologize for disturbing him, but he shook his head and pressed a fingertip against her lips to silence her.

She attempted to stay awake, but fatigue repeatedly claimed her as he sat beside her in the semi-darkness of her bedroom. She didn't admit that the safety and security of his presence faded once her dreams reclaimed her. There were some battles she felt destined to fight alone.

As she showered and then dressed in casual clothes on the second afternoon of their stay in San Francisco, Leah vividly recalled the feel of Brett's fingers sweeping up the side of her face and across her forehead. Her memory of the gentle way he pushed aside her bangs and checked the shrinking bump near her hairline had the power, even now, to send heat streaming into her veins and make her heart thud wildly in her chest. She recalled closing her hands into fists, determined not to touch him or to make him uncomfortable, when all she'd really wanted to do was to sink her fingers into the dark hair that covered his bare, muscled chest and explore every centimeter of his anatomy at her leisure.

Even now she wanted his uniquely masculine taste on her lips, his tongue intruding into her mouth with tantalizing stabs, and his hands roaming the hills and hollows of her naked body. She craved everything about him, his sturdiness, his enticing heat, the tender strength she knew she would find in his embrace, and the sensual pleasure of his maleness buried deep within her.

Shaken by the erotic images flooding her mind and stimulating her senses, Leah closed her eyes. She gripped her hairbrush until her fingers ached, slowly inhaling and exhaling in order to calm herself. Although she couldn't recall ever feeling so aroused by the mere thought of a man, she felt certain that she'd never before experienced such soul-shattering need for anyone.

Several minutes passed before her heartbeat slowed and she regained complete control over herself. Leah glanced in the mirror and took a final look at her reflection as she set aside her hairbrush. Despite having grown familiar with her appearance, she still viewed herself as a partial stranger.

Squaring her shoulders, she turned away from the sink and left the bathroom. She again wore casual clothes and athletic shoes. Given the precise fit of the attire, she now believed that the contents of the suitcases belonged to her.

As she crossed the bedroom, Leah paused to draw open the drapes and collect from the bedside table one of the three photographs she'd been studying for the last day and a half. Something inside her ached with response every time she looked at the photo, and as she left the room, she promised herself that she would discover why.

Leah spotted Brett the instant she walked into the sitting room. Standing in the threshold of the French doors that led out onto the awning-covered balcony of the suite, he appeared to be enjoying the view of the bay despite the cloud-filled spring sky.

When he turned to look at her, she saw relief and something she couldn't quite name in his eyes. Forcing a smile to her lips, she announced. "I've decided to quit hibernating. Whatever happens in the days and weeks ahead, I'm ready to deal with it."

Leah met Brett in the center of the spacious room. She experienced a moment of guilt for having subjected him to long hours of silent brooding, but she sensed that he understood. She welcomed the power she felt in his large hands and long, blunt-tipped fingers as he gripped her shoulders. Looking up at him, she trembled beneath his touch.

"Welcome back, Leah Holbrook. You finally sound like your old self."

"Old, or new, I'm tired of hiding."

"You weren't hiding. You were just coming to terms with what's happened to you. In fact, you've handled this situation the way you've handled tough times in the past. You got off the proverbial merry-go-round and gave yourself a chance to clear your head, because you were smart enough to realize that fear will eat you alive if you don't confront it head-on."

She laughed at his summary of her supposedly rational behavior. "You may be giving me more credit than I deserve."

"No way," he disagreed, his fingers snugly curled over her shoulders, his eyes darker than midnight as he peered down at her.

"I know I might never remember my life, but I want to try. I'll need your help and your memories."

"Anything else?"

She nodded, tears unexpectedly stinging her eyes. "A lot of hugs, a ton of patience, which you obviously have, and the answers to a thousand and one questions."

She went willingly into his arms as he gathered her close, her need to be enveloped in his embrace eclipsing everything else for the moment. Sighing, she savored the power of his large, hard body molded to hers. "Are you sure you're up to this?" she asked several minutes later.

"Stupid question," Brett muttered as he eased his hold on her and brought his hands up to cup her face. "There isn't anything I wouldn't do for you. All you have to do is ask, and it's yours."

She couldn't speak. The tears stinging her eyes pooled and blurred her vision. She turned away from him and wandered in the direction of the couch. Sinking down onto it, she took a moment to harness her emotions. "Sorry. My feelings are quite close to the surface right now."

"Don't apologize, Leah. It comes with the territory, I suspect. Does your head still hurt?" he asked as he joined her on the couch, tugged her against his body, and encircled her shoulders with his arm.

Leah heard his worry and could have kicked herself for acting like such a baby. "The headache's gone, and my bruises are quite colorful now. Despite the sporadic way I've been sleeping, I actually feel pretty good."

"That's what I wanted to hear."

"Are you always so patient?" she asked, still amazed by his willingness to treat her with such an enormous amount of compassion and understanding. Leah realized how much easier it would have been for him to turn her over to her family in Seattle so that they would have the responsibility of handling her problems.

"Hardly," he muttered.

"I've been a royal pain, and you know it."

"Well, maybe, but you're usually pretty together. You're allowed periodic lapses."

"Do we have to stay here much longer?" she asked.

"Of course not. You aren't a prisoner, Leah. I just

wanted to make sure you had a chance to rest. Now that your headache's gone, we can leave anytime. Tomorrow, in fact, if you'd like."

"I'd like," she said enthusiastically.

"Don't like the accommodations, huh?" he groused.

"The suite is beautiful. I just hate feeling like a shut-in."

He chuckled. "You've always had a craving for wide-open spaces."

"Then I'm behaving in character?"

"It looks and sounds that way to me."

"That's encouraging, isn't it?" she asked as she twisted her torso into him in order to get a better view of his face.

Her breasts immediately plumped against his chest, her nipples tightening into pointed buds. Fascinated by Brett's response to her innocent movement, her eyes widened with surprise. Leah unconsciously held her breath, watching as a muscle ticked in his jaw and feeling the dig of his fingers in her shoulder. His strong-featured face looked more dangerous than usual.

She finally found the good sense to pull back a little, but Brett stopped her the instant she began to lean away from him. She felt the flex and flow of the muscles in his upper body as he jerked her against his chest and held her still.

Leah stared at him, her senses enflamed even more by the ragged sound of air being dragged into his lungs and the harsh look on his face. She felt seared all over by the hot glow of his dark gaze, just as she'd felt ready to go up in flames during their first hours together.

He muttered a low, lethal-sounding word before he warned, "Quit rubbing up against me like a cat that craves petting, or you'll get more than you bargained for. I like the feel of you in my arms, just as I'd like nothing better than to strip you naked and bury myself in your hot little body. If you keep this up, Leah, all my good intentions will go up in smoke, and we'll both live to regret it."

Humbled and a little embarrassed by his bluntness, Leah said nothing. She simply nodded. She wanted to be close to him. She wanted to feel his strength and tap into his seemingly bottomless well of innate courage. As well, she needed the reassurance she experienced when he held her. She quelled her desire for anything more, although she didn't expect her longing to know him intimately ever really to end. Not when she knew that he desired her too.

Brett leaned back and closed his eyes. Leah heard him exhale raggedly as she rested her head against his shoulder. Several minutes ticked by before she felt the tension start to drain from both their bodies.

"Were we ever married?" she asked unexpectedly.

Brett flinched as though he'd been struck. "No, Leah, never."

She frowned, oddly disappointed to realize that they weren't lovers and had never been married. Baffled by the strong emotional currents that flowed between them, she sensed that Brett was keeping something very important from her. She made a silent vow to continue her exploration of their complex relationship.

"I want to know everything about you, Brett."

"There isn't much to tell."

She heard a note of wariness in his voice and decided to pursue it. "But it might help trigger memories of my own life if you familiarize me with things about yourself that I've no doubt heard before."

"Sounds like a roundabout way of getting to the truth, but I'll tell you anything I can."

"Good. We'll tackle that side of the situation later. Right now, though, I need to know about one of the children in the picture taken at Yellowstone."

She pulled the photograph in question out of her pocket and showed it to him, waiting while he inspected it.

"Have you remembered something?" Brett asked quietly.

"Nothing," Leah admitted. "But the little boy sitting next to me in the photo is the one child I keep zeroing in on, despite the fact that there are more than ten children gathered around me. He's so serious-looking, almost as though he's worried that I won't remember him. My heart aches when I look at him. The link I feel to this child is just too strong to ignore, Brett, even though I can't offer a rational explanation of why I feel so connected to him."

"You know him quite well."

"Why? How?"

"He's my son, Leah."

"How stupid of me! I should have guessed. He looks like a miniature version of you. He's a very special little boy, isn't he?" She smoothed shaking fingertips down the side of the photograph. "Am I close to him?"

"Extremely."

"How old is he? What's his name?"

"Matthew is going to be six on his next birthday."

"I feel the need to take him into my arms and hold him every time I look at this picture," she confessed. "It's as if he's a very important part of me."

"I'm not at all surprised by your reaction to him.

You'll understand your feelings about him when your memory returns, which it will."

"He's a serious little guy, isn't he?" She glanced up at Brett and smiled, but her smile faded when she felt the tension tightening his body. "Kind of like his father."

He nodded, his gaze narrowing. "So I've been told."

"Do I like children in general, or just your son?"

"You once told me you'd like to have half a dozen."

"Sounds like a lot of work in the labor room." Returning her gaze to the photo, Leah asked, "Where is he now?"

"With his grandparents. They've taken him to Canada for a week of fishing."

"He likes to fish?" Her expression brightened. "Brett, I like to fish too. I'm certain of it."

He smiled down at her. "You taught him how to bait his first hook, and you gave him his first fishing pole."

"Do you see him often? Does he live with you?"

"Unfortunately I don't see nearly enough of him. He doesn't live with me, but I wish he did."

"He's with his mother, then." Leah felt his nod when his chin bobbed against the top of her head. "That must be hard for you. Being divorced, I mean."

"We weren't married when Matthew was born. Actually we were never married. It was a complicated situation, and it's an even more complicated story." He shifted, suggesting, "How about we save this part of my life story for another time."

She eased free of his encircling arm and turned so that she wound up facing him. When her knee bumped against his hip, he absently brought his hand down atop it as he stared off into space. She shivered as his fingers drifted up and down the top of her jeans-covered upper leg, and she wondered what he was thinking as he touched her.

"I didn't mean to make you feel sad."

Brett blinked and refocused on her. "You didn't, although some trips down memory lane tend to remind me of the mistakes I've made with my life and with the people I care about."

"It sounds like you're still carrying a torch for Matthew's mother." Leah felt her heart sink, discovering in the process that she hated the idea that he might be in love with another woman. If Brett still loved little Matthew's mother, she certainly didn't want to hear him admit it. At least not now.

"I have a lot of mixed feelings where she's concerned. We parted before I knew about her pregnancy. I found out quite by accident. I was almost completely cut out of my son's life. It took time and patience, but I eventually discovered a way to be a part of it."

"Didn't you resent her?"

Brett exhaled, the sound harsh in the quiet of the sitting room. "As I said, my emotions were pretty mixed. A part of me understood her behavior. I'd hurt her very badly, and then I walked out on her. Hell, I hold myself responsible for a lot of the decisions she made, but I still wish she'd been willing to tell me the truth when she learned she was pregnant. I would have supported her in any way I could."

"I can't imagine going off and having a baby on my own. I think she was a fool not to come to you and let you share the experience with her."

"She had her reasons," he remarked, his tone faintly defensive. "At the time I'm sure she thought she was right. I have no business faulting her anyway. I've made too many mistakes myself."

Startled by the field of emotions reflected in Brett's eyes, Leah covered his hand with her own. She bit back a yelp of surprise when she felt his fingers flex and then dig into her thigh. She stroked the back of his hand, trying to help him relax in spite of her desire simply to put her arms around him and hold him.

Searching his troubled gaze, Leah realized how easy it would be to drown in the dark depths of his eyes. She felt that she was finally beginning to grasp the complex nature of their relationship, and she sensed that the events of the last few days were probably just a ripple in the pond of their shared experiences.

"I know you very well, don't I, even though you're an intensely private man?"

He nodded. "Better than anyone ever has."

"You remind me of a puzzle," Leah admitted.

"You've said that to me more times than I can count."

Eager to dispel his melancholy mood, she teased, "Was I laughing or shouting?"

He gave her a wry look. "Both, as I recall."

"We must have a roller-coaster relationship."

"I'm sure a lot of people think so."

"Do you?" she asked softly.

Brett cocked his head to one side, peering at her almost speculatively. "We've definitely been up and down over the years."

"Does that bother you?"

Easing away from her, he got to his feet. "Some of the time."

Leah caught his hand when he reached out to her. He tugged her to her feet, surprising her when he wrapped his arms around her and buried his face in the curve of her neck.

Trembling, she slipped her arms around his waist and held on to him. She breathed in his scent, savoring his woodsy cologne and the musky, male essence of his skin. Her eyes fluttered closed. She listened to the steady beat of his heart. When Brett straightened a few minutes later, she reluctantly accepted his withdrawal.

He cupped the side of her face with his hand. "I don't see myself trading you in on a new model, so I guess you're stuck with me."

"Does that mean you've forgiven me for being lousy company?"

He frowned, his consternation with her obvious. Leaning down, he planted a hard kiss on her lips. "I'll think about it."

Leah grinned, her lips still tingling from his kiss. "You must have legions of women beating a path to your door."

"Where'd you get a crazy idea like that?" Brett demanded.

"Chalk it up to a woman's intuition," she suggested. "Your bedside manner is splendid, and you're very attractive, in a rough sort of way."

"That hit you took on your head has distorted your vision and damaged your intellect."

She rolled her eyes, purposely acting silly. "I didn't say you were pretty. Besides, I don't like pretty men. They spend too much time in front of the mirror admiring themselves."

"Any other warped observations before we close this subject permanently?"

"You're also dangerously sexy. Makes a woman go a little crazy when she's with that kind of man."

"Have I just received a warning?"

Leah shrugged, her smile lifting the edges of her mouth. "Maybe, maybe not." She sighed in sudden frustration, all her humor disappearing like a wisp of smoke. "I wish I could remember you. I wish I could remember us."

"You will. I'm just part of a temporary lapse."

"I want to believe you, Brett, but sometimes I wonder if my past is permanently gone."

"Trust me, Leah. You'll get it all back."

She nodded, even though she didn't share his optimism. When he seized her hands and tugged her forward, she eagerly moved back into the safe harbor of his embrace. Leah pressed her cheek to his hard chest, realizing with a flash of insight that she was falling in love with him. She wondered if this was her first time, or if she'd always been in love with Brett.

Six

"I'm feeling really cooped up," Leah confessed several hours later. "Since it's raining, why don't we take a cab over to Fisherman's Wharf? Perhaps we could have supper at one of the restaurants there. Maybe I'll see something familiar that will stimulate my memory. Lord knows, nothing else has so far."

Brett glanced up from the road map he was studying, his expression a combination of caution and regret. "No can do, I'm afraid. I'm expecting a call from Washington."

She sighed, her disappointment apparent. "Then I'll take a walk downstairs. The hotel probably has several boutiques. I can window-shop for a while, and you can join me after you've gotten your call."

Heading for her bedroom to collect her purse, Leah hesitated when Brett set aside the map, left his chair, and blocked her path. She thought she saw a flicker of concern in his eyes, but he quickly hid it.

"Be sensible, Leah. You're not ready to declare your independence and go charging off on your own. How about a picnic supper on the balcony instead?"

77

"How about a picnic supper on the balcony and then a leisurely stroll around the hotel lobby?" she countered. "I need to get out of this suite before I start climbing the walls."

"Let's see how you feel after we've eaten," he suggested. Brett walked to the desk on the opposite side of the room, picked up the room-service menu that rested next to the telephone, and gave it to her once she joined him. "Why don't you order for us? You love seafood, and so do I."

She gripped the menu. "I must be mildly claustrophobic, and I definitely feel cranky."

He smiled at her. "To use your words, you're just feeling cooped up, that's all. Don't be so hard on yourself, but do try to be a little more patient. We'll be leaving tomorrow morning. The doctor said the first forty-eight hours were a critical time for you. She's the expert, so we're going to bow to her judgment in this situation. All right?"

She nodded reluctantly. She knew Brett was just trying to protect her, but she still chafed at the necessity of such behavior. "Agreed."

Brett ran his knuckles down the side of her face. "That's my girl."

Leah turned her face and pressed her lips to his knuckles. She felt a tremor pass through Brett's fingers. Glancing at him, she thought she saw hunger and desire in his dark eyes. Leah let the menu fall to the floor. She caught his hand, which had become a clenched fist, before he could withdraw it, pried open his fingers one by one, and pressed a gentle kiss into his palm.

"Leah . . ." he began.

"Brett, please don't say anything. Just listen to me for a moment." Looking up at him, she searched his face for understanding, but she glimpsed only raw need before he finally nodded. "All I have right now are my instincts. When I touch you, I feel as though I'm behaving in the most natural way possible. When I try to restrain myself, I feel as though someone's thrown away the key to my heart. You've been very understanding and gentle with me," she continued. "You've also provided me with a safety net I wouldn't otherwise have if I tried to deal with my memory loss alone, but I think you've discovered feelings in yourself for me that you aren't sure how to handle, so you're denying your own emotions in an effort to help me and protect me. Please stop doing that. It's driving me crazy, and it's not fair to either one of us."

His expression bleak, he insisted, "You don't understand what you're saying."

"You're wrong. I know exactly what I'm saying, so quit being so circumspect about everything you say and do. There's no need. I will never criticize you or condemn you or accuse you of taking advantage of me, regardless of what we share or don't share, and whether or not my memory returns. Clear?"

She didn't turn away from his probing gaze. She simply waited for him to accept or reject her words. She knew she had no other choice. If there was a woman in his life, he owed her the truth now. If not, then he owed them both the honesty of his own emotions. Leah prayed that he grasped her sincerity, not just the decision she'd made about her desire to allow their relationship to evolve without impediments.

"I meant it when I told you I didn't want you ever to reach a point when you considered me a mistake in judgment. I care enough about you to want you to have the happiness you deserve."

"What about you?" she asked. "What would make you happy?"

"You make me happy, Leah. You always have."

She moved forward into his arms, which encompassed her with startling speed. Molding herself against his body, she rested her head against his chest. "Is there someone else?" she asked, even though she feared his answer.

He gripped her upper arms and gave her a little shake. Surprised, she peered up at him. "Does that mean there isn't?"

"How can you even ask?"

"Then don't shy away from me when I touch you, and don't fight your feelings," she whispered. "Please don't push me away anymore, Brett, because it makes me feel empty inside when you do."

"I'm still not going to take you into my bed for the wrong reasons and under the wrong circumstances," he muttered fiercely. "There are things you don't remember about me. Things you deserve to know. I'm not such a bastard that I'd deprive you of the right to make an informed decision about the kind of man I am, Leah."

"You're a man with a conscience, Brett Upton."

"I thought so a long time ago, but I know better now."

She smiled as she stepped away and retrieved the menu she'd allowed to fall to the floor. "I guess I'll have to prove you wrong, won't I?"

"Good luck."

Leah watched Brett rake careless fingers through his thick dark hair as he turned away and returned to his chair. Slouching down in it, he grabbed the map he'd discarded earlier and stared at it.

Leah smiled as she dialed the number for hotel room service, aware that she'd finally made a dent in his constant restraint. Instinct and the emotions Brett stirred in her compelled her, she realized, to bring down the walls that kept them apart. She didn't intend to fail.

A waiter delivered a room-service cart filled with covered dishes that contained crabmeat cocktails, Caesar salad for two, broiled lobster tails with drawn butter, sourdough bread, and two slices of cheese-cake. Brett barely allowed the bewildered young man to step into the suite before collecting the check, signing it, and sending him on his way with a generous tip. The waiter was still offering to uncork a bottle of white wine from a well-known Napa Valley vintner that Leah had ordered when Brett closed and locked the suit door.

"I don't like sharing you," he told Leah when he noticed her chagrined expression.

"You're hopeless."

"Where you're concerned, that's truer than you know."

They adjourned to the awning-covered balcony despite the misting rain. Brett pulled a small table and two chairs away from the railing and positioned them against the exterior wall of the suite after drying them with a towel. A sniper, even one with a powerful night scope, would be hard-pressed, he knew, to turn Leah into a target once he seated her in the most protected spot on the balcony. He felt satisfied that she would be able to see the cloud-filled sky and a periodic star, while no one would see her. Attired in heavy sweaters to ward off the chill of the damp night air, they ate their meal and chatted.

"I think we should kidnap the chef," Leah commented after groaning her pleasure over their meal.

Recalling the event that had almost robbed him of Leah and their son of his mother, Brett paled at her innocent remark. He pushed aside the plate that held his dessert, what remained of his appetite disappearing. Sinking back in his chair, he absently sipped his wine.

"You're very quiet all of a sudden," Leah remarked after eating the last bite of her cheesecake.

Brett voiced the first thought that entered his head. "I was thinking about how different we are."

She smiled. "I assume you're speaking of things other than the obvious anatomical differences."

He nodded, but he didn't smile back at her. Instead he silently pondered the contents of his wineglass, his thoughts centered on Leah and what it would be like to experience her passion again after so many years. Brett felt the change in his body almost immediately, and he cursed his lack of control as desire unfurled in his veins like hot ribbons of flame.

"Tell me about your family, Brett," Leah encouraged. "You've hardly said a word about your past, and you promised you would."

"There's nothing to tell," he said, his tone abrupt.

"Of course there is."

"I didn't have a family, at least not like yours. I was placed in foster care before I was old enough to walk. I grew up in a variety of homes, some good, some not so good. I lucked out with the last family that took me in while I was in high school. They were retired navy. My grades and my athletic ability were above average, so Bob Stoner, my foster father, helped me apply to the Naval Academy. Much to everyone's amazement, I received a congressional appointment. The rest, as they say, is history."

"History I don't know," she reminded him as she set aside her empty wineglass. Curling her legs beneath her, she studied him for a long moment. "What happened to your parents?"

"I don't know anything about them. I was abandoned shortly after birth." Brett shrugged. "Whoever they were, they gave me life and a name that was written on a slip of paper and pinned to my blanket. I took it from there."

Leah looked genuinely stunned. "How terrifying!"

"Not really. I was too young to know that my life wasn't normal when I was being passed from one foster family to another. By the time I did figure it out, I was old enough to realize that there are some things you can't change."

"You understand better than anyone how disconnected I feel, don't you?"

Brett nodded, his face empty of expression. "I have a pretty good idea."

"Is the lack of emotional security in your childhood one of the reasons that you like my family so much?" she asked.

He felt unsettled by her question, but he was willing to be honest with her. "I've always envied the closeness." As he spoke, he realized that he'd never been this truthful with Leah before. "I'd never seen anything like it. At first I didn't believe it was real."

"What convinced you?"

"Being welcomed into the Holbrook family circle without question or hesitation," he answered simply. "Your parents treated me like one of their own." *And then I repaid them,* he recalled bitterly, *by turning their daughter into an unwed mother and my own son into a bastard.*

"You said we met in Washington, D.C., courtesy of my eldest brother, right?"

Brett nodded. "I'd been to Seattle with Micah a few

times during our academy days, but you were away at school during our visits."

"So we met in Washington."

He nodded, remembering the immediate and intense chemistry they'd shared. "You were living with Micah while you did a political-science internship as a congressional aide during your senior year of college. You were subsequently offered the same job when you graduated, and you moved into one of the spare rooms at Micah's."

She looked confused. "How in the world did I wind up co-owning a flower shop in Monterey?"

"You wanted a change," he said carefully. "You don't suffer fools easily, Leah. You never have. You once told me you'd grown to loathe the jaded attitudes and personalities of the power brokers who worked in the upper echelons of government. Sarah Kelly's husband died a few years after you accepted the job with Congressman Hardiman. She was in danger of losing the flower shop and needed a partner to keep it solvent. You'd had enough of backroom politics, so you took your savings, packed everything you owned, and made the cross-country move. You left a note for Micah, because we were in Europe on an assignment. You didn't look back."

"I sound very decisive, but it can't have been that simple."

He smiled grimly. "You've always been decisive. The people who know and understand you don't expect you to change. As for the decision you made to leave Washington, everything happened within the space of a few weeks."

"Were we good friends even then?" she asked.

"The three of us, plus whoever Micah happened to be seeing at the time, spent all our off-duty time together. Trips to the shore, picnics, skiing, and concerts. That kind of thing." He saw her frown. Although he sensed that she didn't believe his cursory description of their past, he didn't feel that this was the right time to provide her with a detailed description of their love affair or their broken engagement.

"Sounds wonderful."

"It was a really good time," he agreed, his emotions shielded behind an even expression. Listening to the rain intensify in force, Brett unexpectedly recalled Leah's passion for long walks in the warm summer rain, usually after they'd spent a lazy Sunday afternoon making love in the privacy of his small Arlington, Virginia, apartment.

"Do you like your work in law enforcement?" she asked.

He blinked and refocused on her. Once again, Brett proceeded with caution. "I'm on the move a lot, both in the United States and abroad."

"Sounds fascinating."

He passed a hand across his eyes, his fingertips lingering at the bridge of his nose as he massaged the ache there. "I really can't talk about it, except in general terms. Most of what I do is highly classified. The people I deal with aren't your run-of-the-mill criminals. They don't knock over the corner bank or rob the liquor store on the wrong side of town. They mount revolutions and take over countries, and they don't give a damn how many lives they destroy in the process."

Leah leaned forward, rested her elbows on the edge of the table, and propped her chin in her palms. She studied him for a long moment. "I don't mean to pry, but chasing criminals around the globe has to wear a person down after a while. Doesn't it get to you? I can't even begin to imagine what it must be like for you to be constantly alert to any possible threat that might come your way."

Leave it to Leah, he thought, to pinpoint and articulate an important part of his frustration with the evil, violence-filled world he inhabited. "It's not quite that intense."

Brett got to his feet and walked to the edge of the balcony. After peering first left, then right, he studied the lighted rooftop of the building situated across from their hotel. As he stood there, he gripped the railing with both hands and tried to banish the images of death and destruction that filled his mind.

While he'd once derived satisfaction from tracking down and jailing terrorists of every stripe, he now felt emotionally bankrupt from the years he'd spent groveling in the sewers of the world. And because he'd immersed himself in the identity of an extremist capable of murder, he knew he carried the taint of those years. He suspected he always would.

"How can it not be?" Leah asked. "Intense, I mean. If these people are as deadly as you've implied, then you're at risk all the time, aren't you?"

"Anyone who does what I do is at risk. It's part of the job description. When you can't take it anymore, you get the hell out. Otherwise, you jeopardize yourself and the people you're responsible for."

"Brett . . ."

He turned to find her standing beside him. Alarm bells went off in his head. Starved for her compassion, but also desperate to keep her safe, he slipped his arm around her with as much calm as he could muster, and led her away from the railing and back under the awning.

"Have I touched a nerve?" she asked gently.

He gave her a tight smile as he steadily moved them in the direction of the entrance to the suite.

"Perhaps, but I know it wasn't intentional, so don't worry about it."

She paused, still in the circle of his arm, and looked up at him. "Your work is extremely dangerous, probably life-threatening."

Unprepared for the worry he saw in her eyes and heard in her voice, Brett quelled his desire to drag her into his bed and submerge himself in the volatility of her passion. He needed her so much that his soul ached. Despite what she'd said earlier, he knew she'd hate him once she regained her memory of him if he allowed himself to indulge his hunger for her. "At times," he conceded.

"What you *aren't* saying is feeding my imagination."

He heard large raindrops splatter angrily across the awning above their heads. The sound reminded him of rounds being fired from an automatic weapon. "Let's go inside now."

Leah didn't protest. She simply went along with him, her expression still filled with worry. He kept his arm around her as he secured the door and closed the drapes.

Raindrops sparkled like diamonds in her golden hair, which she'd fashioned into a elegant French braid. Brett used his fingertips to smooth away a droplet of water caught just below the seam of her lips. He felt a warm gust of air escape her. He also saw her surprise that he'd touched her so intimately in the widening of her blue-green eyes. Shaken by the play of emotions in her expressive features, he lowered his hand and closed it into a fist, willing himself not to touch her again.

"You don't like your life very much, do you, Brett? And you aren't happy, are you?"

Startled by her perceptiveness, he insisted, "It has its moments."

"Don't lie to me," she said, a combative note in her voice. "Your eyes are positively bleak when you talk about your work."

"I've been chasing bad guys for a long time, Leah. You get used to it."

"Or burned out," she suggested sadly. "Is that what's happened to you? Is that one of the reasons we decided to take a vacation together? Did you need some time out of the line of fire in order to decide what you wanted to do in the future?"

He attempted a smile, but he produced a grimace instead. "Been reading my mind again?" he tried to joke, but his voice lacked even a hint of humor.

She gripped his forearms. "I'm so sorry, Brett. I've turned into an unexpected burden when you needed my understanding and support. Maybe you should put me on a plane. I can fly up to Seattle . . ."

He jerked her forward, his arms like bands of steel around her as he molded her against his solid body. Leah stared up at him, shock and something more in her expression.

Brett glared at her with eyes that burned with a combination of fever and fury. "You're not a damn burden, so get that idiotic thought out of your head right now."

"How can I not be?" she cried, trying to twist free of him.

Brett tensed, responding instantly to her struggle and the feel of her shapely body moving against him. He felt every seductive inch of her, and he died a little inside because he knew his life was cursed without her.

His restraint snapped. He grabbed her hips and held her still. Shifting his pelvis forward, he rubbed against the cradle of her thighs. Brett groaned, the sound raw as it emerged from his throat. Heat sizzled in his veins, drove his heart into a furious gallop, and challenged his ability to control the surging power in his loins. Throwing back his head, he closed his eyes and ground his jaws together. He fought for control, but he knew he'd already lost the battle.

Leah held her breath as she lifted her arms and looped them around his neck. Tugging his head down, she enflamed his senses even more when she swept the tip of her tongue back and forth across his lower lip.

Brett felt a near-violent tremor of hunger rip through his body, almost as though he'd been trapped in the epicenter of an earthquake.

Leah clasped his head with both hands and teased his lips apart. Dipping her tongue past his even teeth and into his mouth, she moaned as she took her first taste of him.

His conscience abandoning him, Brett responded to Leah. He felt her hands trail down the sides of his neck, across his shoulders, and then pause as she flattened her palms against his chest. His heart thudded with devastating force, his senses exploding in the wake of the tantalizing trail of flame induced by her tongue as she explored his mouth.

He gripped her hips more tightly, telling himself that he had to put an end to this exquisite torture, but he couldn't muster the strength or the will to draw away from Leah, who even now undulated against the hard ridge of flesh that proclaimed his desire for her. Capturing her tongue, he sucked it deeper into his mouth and tenderly trapped it with his teeth. Brett inhaled her breathless sighs and reveled in the possessive feel of her hands when she frantically worked her fingertips beneath his black turtleneck sweater.

Sensation after sensation assaulted him. His hands shook, his heart raced like a locomotive, and the muscles in his thighs burned. He felt her fingers sink into and then comb through the dark pelt of hair that covered his chest.

Somehow, they wound up on the floor, kneeling thigh to thigh, hip to hip, and chest to breasts. Seemingly of one mind, they simultaneously stripped themselves of their sweaters.

Brett traced Leah's delicate collarbone before gently placing his fingertip against the pulse that throbbed in the hollow of her throat. Fascinated by the rapid pace of her pulse, the flushed beauty and fragrance of her ginger-scented skin, and the look of glazed passion that filled her eyes, he allowed his gaze to fall to her breasts.

"You are so exquisite," he whispered as he freed the catch and peeled her white-lace bra away from her body.

Tight, dark-coral nipples crowned her breasts and stabbed into the center of his palms as he fitted his hands over her flesh. He shuddered when he felt her satiny heat, his fingers spasming as he held her. "I've dreamed of touching you this way."

In response Leah arched into his hands and pressed her lips to his chin. Trailing her fingers down his hard, flat stomach, she slipped them past the waistband of his black trousers even as she opened her mouth to his intruding tongue.

Brett's stomach muscles clenched under the glide of her fingers. Leah sighed shakily. He drank in the sound as he smoothed his fingers back and forth across her distended nipples.

She was fuller now and her nipples were darker,

he realized as he caught her by the waist, lifted her until her chest was level with his lips, and then pressed a hot, open-mouthed kiss into the scented valley that separated her breasts. He felt her nails dig into his shoulders as he closed his mouth over the coral tip of one breast.

She whispered his name over and over again. Lost in the erotic sound of her voice, he fed his hunger for her as he sipped at her breasts and then tugged at her nipples with gentle teeth. All the while he knew that the desire that had gnawed at his soul for six long years wouldn't be even partially appeased until he'd buried himself in the depths of her heated flesh.

"I want you," Leah pleaded.

Brett slowly lowered her until until her knees touched the carpet. Both breathless and shaking, they stared at each other. He loosened her braid, his fingers clumsy but determined as he unwove it and then shoved is hands into the dense golden silk that tumbled all the way to her waist.

Kneading her scalp with his fingers, he claimed her mouth, felt the frantic movement of her hands as she tried to touch him everywhere at once, and absorbed the hectic pace of her heartbeat as it branded his naked chest.

The feel of her fingers tugging at the zipper of his trousers finally penetrated his sensual greed. Brett seized Leah's wrists and dragged her hands away from his body.

He muttered an ugly word, damning himself to hell for being such a fool. Tremors of desire and despair continued to war within him. His desire began to ease, almost like a reluctantly departing tide. His despair triumphed soon after, forcing him to face the predictable consequences of careless passion. He knew Leah would never forgive him if he took her now. And he would never forgive himself.

"Don't stop me," she whispered as she tried to wrench free of his grasp.

He shook his head, refusing to release her until he persuaded her to listen to him. "You'll hate me forever if we do this," he insisted.

"Don't stop us, Brett."

The shattered look of disbelief etched into her features fueled the contempt he felt for himself. "I have to," he said, his voice so raw that he didn't even recognize the sound of it.

"Damn you," she breathed, shaking as she jerked free of him and reached for her clothes. A single tear crept down her cheek. "Damn you."

"I already am."

Leah held her sweater against her breasts as she got to her feet and made her way to the nearest chair. She sank into it, closed her eyes, and breathed slowly in and out in an obvious effort to regain control over herself.

Brett flinched and forced his gaze away from her white-knuckled grip on her sweater. He pulled himself up from the floor and staggered to a chair on the opposite side of the room. His entire body burned.

"I've got to stop touching you," he remarked quietly a few minutes later.

Leah opened her eyes and stared at him for a long, intense moment. "If you do, I'll never forgive you."

"Leah . . ."

She waved him into silence. The sweater dipped, revealing one of her hard-nippled breasts. Brett ground his jaws together and dug his fingers into the arms of his chair.

"Don't tell me I don't understand. I don't want to hear it."

"One of us has to think clearly."

"I trust my heart. Maybe you should try doing the same thing," she suggested, her tone belligerent enough to make her sound as though she was preparing for combat. "I also trust you in everything but this attraction we feel for each other. You've got the instincts of a rock where I'm concerned, because you aren't wise enough to trust me to know what I need and want. I may not have a memory, but I understand my feelings. Why don't you check out your own? If you don't want me, say so. But if you do, then admit it and call off this blasted game you're playing with our emotions. We'll both be crippled for life if you don't stop pushing me away."

"You can't afford an attitude like that, Leah."

"I'll afford anything I damn well please, Brett Upton. Anything!"

She stood abruptly, her sweater falling away from her breasts. She caught it and let it hang from her fingers as she faced him. Making no effort to conceal her naked upper body from his burning gaze, she slowly crossed the room, her spine rigid, her breasts gently, enticingly swaying with every step she took, and her head held high.

Once again, Brett grappled with the changes that had taken place in Leah during their years apart. Assertive and independent, she obviously understood herself, even without the benefit of knowing the facts of the previous thirty years of her life. And once again, he felt like a fool for underestimating her.

"Leah?"

She paused in the open doorway of her bedroom, but she didn't turn around.

His gaze riveted on the oddly patterned bruise that started beneath her armpit and disappeared from view into the waistband of her belted jeans, Brett swallowed the choking fury that made him want to deal personally with the men who'd harmed her.

"I'm still waiting," she said with a subdued dignity that made her seem that much more vulnerable.

"We're leaving early in the morning. You'll want to be packed and ready by six."

She nodded.

Covering his face with his hands, Brett kneaded his forehead with his fingers and silently applauded Leah for not slamming her bedroom door.

Seven

As they traveled north on Route 101, Brett ended several hours of silence late the next morning when he asked, "Would you prefer a seafood restaurant when we stop for lunch, or would a cheeseburger, fries, and a milk shake hit the spot?"

Leah shrugged, her thoughts on the photograph she was studying. "I trust your judgment. Whatever appeals to you is fine with me." She lifted her gaze from the group photo taken following her sister's wedding a few minutes later and looked at Brett. Sculpted by an unforgiving Creator, his hard-cheeked, strong-boned profile continued to fascinate her.

"You're staring."

She teased, "It doesn't pay to deny the obvious, so I'll plead guilty and throw myself on the mercy of the court." He glanced in her direction, almost grudgingly, Leah thought. "I do think we need a formal truce if we're going to eat a meal together, though." She caught a fleeting impression of his surprise before he returned his attention to the traffic ahead of them.

"Whatever you want, Leah," he finally said.

"What do *you* want?"

"More than I have any right to expect."

"We could start our truce by declaring an end to cryptic remarks like that one."

Brett flicked yet another glance at the rearview mirror. His dark, slashing brows shadowed eyes narrowed to slits as he briefly inspected the pickup truck traveling behind them on the road. Frowning, he shifted in his seat and ran his fingertips over the butt of the holstered gun he'd tucked beneath his right thigh.

Observing his behavior, Leah turned in her seat and peered curiously at the late-model truck. "Those two fellows have been with us since we left San Francisco. They must have stopped at the same gas station and rest stops we used. I wonder where they're headed."

"There's no telling," he murmured.

Leah chalked Brett's behavior up to his usual cautionary standards, although she considered his preoccupation with the vehicle behind them unnecessary. She decided that he must be recalling the driver of the truck who'd nearly mowed them down in the clinic parking lot two nights earlier. Determined to brighten his mood, she decided to distract him. "Did I grow up in a rural environment?"

He shot her a quick, startled look. "Part of the time."

"I keep having mental images of playing hide-and-seek in an orchard filled with apple trees."

"Your Dad owns several hundred acres of apple orchards. It's more a hobby than anything else, since he runs his own accounting firm. You once told me that you spent your childhood summers on the farm he inherited from his parents."

"And my mother. Does she work in the medical field?"

Brett nodded. "Helene's an emergency-room nurse. She works part-time."

"Carrie's tenth-birthday party was a disaster," she recalled aloud. "Gavin tried to give his frog swimming lessons in the punch bowl. Micah rescued them both, or they wouldn't have lived to see the next day."

Brett quietly asked, "Any memories of more recent events?"

"No, just early ones. I must be twelve or thirteen in the time frame I'm dealing with right now, because I'm a few years older than Carrie."

"That's great, Leah."

"It's kind of eerie too. I'm seeing myself during my childhood in my mind's eye. Scab-covered knees, long braids, nothing hips, flat-chested and wondering if I'd ever grow breasts. Some of the memories are as clear as a bell, but others are disjointed and remind me of a trip to the twilight zone."

"When did you start remembering?"

"This morning. In the shower, of all places."

He chuckled. "That's as good a place as any, I suppose. What else do you remember?"

She smiled, traveling mentally through a portion of her adolescence that seemed, for the most part, very innocent. "Spending a week in bed when I had the measles. Micah must have been in high school then, probably a senior. He was my hero. He used to sneak cookies up to me when no one was looking, and he'd read to me until I fell asleep at night. I adored him."

"You still do."

"We've stayed close?"

"You two have a special bond. You always have. He calls you his conscience."

Leah looked confused. "I wonder why."

"I think I'll let him tell you."

"He's that wild, huh?"

"Not really. *Unconventional* is probably a better word for Micah. He's always marched to his own drummer. Do your recollections of the past feel like they belong to you?"

Leah thought about his question for a moment before she responded. "Most of them."

Brett reached out and snagged her hand. His gaze continued to travel to the rearview mirror as he navigated the winding road that led to the Oregon border.

Leah welcomed his warm touch and the casual way that he laced their fingers together. Because he'd done his scrupulous best to avoid any physical contact, even innocent contact, since their departure from the hotel early that morning, she felt relieved that they'd finally bridged the gap created by the tension of their sexually charged encounter of the previous night.

A short while later Brett exited the highway. He guided the rental car into a partially filled parking lot in front of a group of stores that offered everything from homemade doughnuts to sporting goods.

Leah spotted the antique shop the instant Brett pulled into a parking space. He turned off the ignition, pocketed his keys, and looked at Leah, the hint of a self-satisfied grin tugging at the edges of his mouth.

She hurriedly unfastened her seatbelt, her fingers clumsy in her haste and excitement. She flashed a smile at Brett, a brilliant smile that made her aquamarine eyes sparkle as she studied the huge sign in front of them that read, COLLECTIBLES. "I love antiques, don't I?"

"Almost as much as you love kids and dogs," he confirmed. "Did you forget about the house you've spent the last four years remodeling?"

She nodded, surprised at herself for neglecting to remember what he'd told her. "I guess I did."

"I need to check under the hood, so why don't you poke around inside? I'll come after you when I'm done."

Leah leaned forward to hug him. Pleasure flooded her senses when he didn't pull away. If anything, she discovered, he seemed inclined to move closer, to actually welcome her touch. She found a world of peace in his embrace, and she let herself bask in the security of it. As well, she loved the feel of his strong hands bracketing her waist, almost as much as she loved the scent of his skin.

"You're a mind reader, Brett Upton," she whispered in his ear before pressing a light kiss to the side of his neck. She felt a tremor run through him a heartbeat before his fingers snugged at her waist. Easing backward, Leah almost tumbled into the depths of his bottomless dark eyes.

"It's good to see you smiling again."

Hearing the ragged quality of his voice and feeling the possessiveness of his hands as they skimmed up and down her back, Leah allowed herself a moment to imagine what it would be like to experience the full force of his passion.

Sensation after sensation shimmied through her body, making her breathless and hungry for him. "You're the cause, so you get to take all the credit." Still smiling, she eased free of him, pushed open her door, and exited the car.

Brett watched her until she was safely inside the

antique shop, aware the entire time that the driver of the pickup truck had followed them into the parking lot. He turned his attention to the two men who'd tracked them since their departure from San Francisco. Although they looked like weekend fishermen as they left their vehicle and stretched their legs in the parking lot, he still felt uneasy about their presence. He didn't intend to tolerate it any longer.

Brett waited, still and watchful, his blood flowing like sluggish rivers of ice through his veins. He observed the two men as they followed Leah into the antique shop after a cursory inspection of the sporting goods store located next door.

Brett moved with stealthy efficiency once the men disappeared from view. Although he disliked leaving Leah alone with them for even a moment, he reminded himself that there were enough people in the antique store to forestall any overt behavior by the two men. Forcing himself to stay calm, he timed his next endeavor to a lull in the traffic flowing into and out of the parking lot.

Satisfied a few minutes later that the men would be delayed indefinitely, Brett made his way into the antique store, where he found Leah chatting with the elderly owner. He managed to contain and conceal his fury, despite the covetous looks on the faces of the two men as they watched Leah. He used patience he didn't even know he possessed to chat with Leah and the shop owner before urging her back into the car.

Leah settled back in the passenger seat and refastened her seatbelt. As they exited the parking lot, she noticed the flat tires on the pickup truck of the two men who'd followed her into the antique shop.

She knew she wouldn't normally question one flat tire, but four of them startled her.

She glanced at Brett, surprise and curiosity in her eyes as she studied him. Although convinced that she was probably being paranoid, she still sensed that he'd had something to do with the disabled pickup. She waited, though, until he eased their rental car into the flow of northbound traffic and they resumed their journey before saying anything.

"Were those men following us?"

Brett kept his eyes on the traffic in front of them. "I'm not sure," he admitted, his grip on the steering wheel tight enough to whiten his knuckles.

Alarmed by his obvious tension, she voiced her speculative thoughts. "But you decided they probably were, and that's why you let the air out of their tires."

He gave her a hard, virtually unreadable look. "I have enemies, Leah."

"There's more to this than 'having enemies,' isn't there? I have a feeling that you're keeping something really important from me." She hesitated, glanced down at the photographs she invariably felt the need to hold, and then peered at Brett. "I get the same unsettling feeling every time I look at this picture taken at Yellowstone. It's almost as though you're keeping a secret from me that everyone else knows. Are you afraid I won't be able to handle the truth if you're honest with me about a recent family tragedy or an incident that involved the two of us at some point in the past?"

Brett paled, but his denial came swiftly. "Of course not, Leah. When the time is right, I promise we'll talk. Bombarding you with information isn't going to help you. For now, we only have one priority. You need to relax enough to let *all* your memories return.

Distractions of any kind will simply interfere with the process. Will you trust me on this?"

Leah said nothing at first. More than anything, she felt the frustration of not knowing enough about herself to refute his reasoning. When Brett glanced at her again, she saw both his conviction that he was doing the right thing and his concern for her.

Still baffled by the reasons for his stubborn behavior, not just annoyed with him and the situation, she exhaled softly and tried to think of a rational explanation for his apparent need to control the flow of information she received. As hard as she tried, she couldn't find one.

"Please trust me," he urged once more, his tone of voice so serious that she almost felt guilty for pressing him. Almost, but not quite.

"I do trust you. I've trusted you from the start," she reminded him, her exasperation evident. "That won't change, Brett. Look, I know I can't force you to reveal what's got you so worried, but I don't believe I'm the kind of woman who'll tolerate being wrapped in cotton batting on an indefinite basis. It doesn't *feel* right. In fact it feels totally wrong, even patronizing at times. Perhaps getting hit on the head has made me a stronger person. I honestly don't know."

"You are strong, Leah. I just didn't always see it."

"I expect the truth, the complete truth, and I won't wait much longer for it, Brett. I've discovered that I don't possess a limitless amount of patience. So, fair warning. The next time I ask a question, I expect a thoroughly honest reply from you. No more dodging reality, and no more half-truths. I'm not a child, and I refuse to be treated like one."

He nodded, his expression grim as he lapsed into an extended silence that lasted as they crossed the state line into Oregon, left the more heavily traveled

Route 101 for a back road to the coast, and stopped for the promised cheeseburgers, fries, and milk shakes at a coffee shop about an hour later in the first coastal town they came to.

Leah remained very watchful of both Brett and their surroundings as they continued north following a silent lunch. She didn't question him when he pulled into a rental-car agency to exchange their vehicle for another nondescript sedan. Neither did she press him for an explanation late that afternoon when he failed to consult her about his decision to check them into a rustic-looking lodge situated atop a high bluff that overlooked the rock-strewn beach and surging, white-capped waters of the Pacific Ocean.

As she got out of the car, Leah thought the lodge looked like a sturdy timber-and-rock fortress. She quickly realized that the building, not just the rugged outcropping of ancient volcanic rock on which it sat, reminded her of Brett.

Convinced that she was growing whimsical, she remained subdued as he escorted her to the top floor at the far end of the main building of the lodge. Their room, spacious and decorated in a pleasantly rustic motif, contained a huge stone fireplace, two double beds, a sitting area, a table and chairs, and a large bathroom that boasted the unexpected luxury of a whirlpool tub.

Leah watched him drop her suitcase on one bed, his own on the second bed. The look he gave her, a steely look that challenged Leah to disagree with his desire to keep his distance from her, made her step back a pace. She stopped herself before she backed all the way out of the room, silently vowing that this moody man, this man whom she loved, wasn't going to intimidate her or deprive her of her desire for him, despite his apparent determination to alienate her completely.

She felt Brett's tension intensify as the weather grew increasingly inclement. When he wasn't brooding or looking out the window to ponder the heavy rain, he paced their room like a caged panther as dusk turned to darkness.

Although she wondered if she should continue to ignore Brett's behavior, Leah cared too much about him to allow him to shut her out much longer. She felt determined to help him relax. Perhaps then, she reasoned silently, he would feel freer to confide in her and provide her with the truths he felt compelled to conceal. Perhaps then, she also prayed, he would allow himself to express his feelings for her.

After freshening up and changing into warmer clothes, Leah joined Brett for the walk down to the small restaurant off the main lobby of the lodge. He persisted in sustaining his role as a silent, watchful sentry while they dined, thus prompting Leah to make her move.

"I've remembered some of the names of my classmates and teachers from the academy I attended in Seattle during high school. I must have been a student there when you visited with Micah. I only got home one weekend a month, so that explains why we didn't meet until I came to Washington."

She smiled at Brett, an innocent smile that should have warned him of the nature of her next comment. "I also remember stuffing my bra with socks for the first boy-girl dance I attended my freshman year. My roommate and I were late bloomers. Unfortunately, one of my socks fell out while I was dancing. Once I figured out that everyone had stopped dancing to stare at my uneven chest, I was totally humiliated. I must have stayed holed up in my dorm room for at least a week after that incident."

Leah laughed at the surprise that flickered in his eyes, the sound of her humor warm and intimate. "It's a miracle my psyche wasn't permanently dented, especially since some twit on the yearbook staff decided to put a picture of an abandoned gym sock next to my graduation photo."

Brett's harsh facade finally cracked. His gaze dipped below her chin for a lingering inspection of her physical attributes. Leah heard the ragged half-sigh, half-laugh that escaped him as he studied the gentle swells beneath her sweater.

"Nature obviously rewarded you for your patience in that department," he observed, his gaze heating as he visually stroked her with his dark eyes.

Her pulse picked up speed. Leah grinned and silently congratulated herself for penetrating the wall of silence he'd erected around himself. She continued to share snippets of her past, primarily recollections from her teenage and early college years, as they lingered over coffee and dessert. They were the last diners in the restaurant when their waitress brought them the check for their meal.

"I almost feel like I'm being deluged by my memories," Leah confided. "There are gaps, of course, but my past is coming back to me. I have to admit that I'm having trouble with some of the chronology, but I'll get the sequence of events straightened out."

As she continued to speak, Leah kept a close eye on Brett's body language, which appeared to be undergoing a subtle transformation. She watched the tension in his face and upper body ease, and she also noticed that he'd stopped gripping the handle of his coffee cup like a weapon. When he smiled at her as she described a humorous escapade from her college days, she managed not to stand up and cheer, although she wanted to.

A short while later he placed two twenty-dollar bills on the table. "It's getting late. Why don't we head back to our room?"

Leah leaned forward, confessing softly, "I'm in need of a hug."

He looked vaguely thoughtful before he nodded. "I think that can be arranged."

"I hate it when we're at odds with each other, Brett. I've felt so lonely all day."

A muscle in his jaw jumped. He reached for her hand and ran the blunt tip of one of his fingers back and forth across her exposed palm. Leah felt his touch in the depths of her soul.

"Me, too, Leah. Me, too," he finally gritted out before releasing her hand and getting to his feet.

She collected her purse and stood. Noting Brett's hesitation, she asked, "Is something wrong?"

"The only thing that's wrong is me. I've behaved like a bastard all day. I owe you an apology."

"An apology isn't necessary," she said. "Just don't treat me as though I'm invisible if you're worried about something or if you're angry with me. Be willing to talk to me, Brett, because when you shut me out, I feel as though I'm dying inside."

Leah welcomed the strong arm he slipped around her shoulders as they left the restaurant, just as she welcomed the warmth and strength of his embrace when they turned out all the lights in their room and settled into the loveseat in front of a roaring fire. Her intuition told her that Brett cared more deeply for her than he was prepared to admit, but she felt no such restrictions on her emotions.

Gathered against his chest, Leah whispered, "I love you," just seconds before the security she found in his embrace and the steady cadence of his heart-beat lulled her to sleep.

I love you.

Her words reverberated within his soul, stunning him, briefly stilling his pulse. Brett hadn't ever expected to hear her utter them again. His heart rocketed into the heavens, but it quickly reversed course and plummeted back to reality. The startling burst of pleasure he'd initially felt died in the space of a single breath, leaving him mired in a state of emotional defeat.

Brett knew better than to let himself believe Leah. She would loathe him when she finally remembered the truth, which he suspected would happen very soon given the almost sequential nature of her returning memory. As well, he cautioned himself against hoping for the impossible—her forgiveness—because life had already taught him that some things can never be forgiven or retrieved.

She would run from him, just as she'd run from him to start a new life in Monterey six years ago. And, he knew, she would hate him even more.

Brett lost track of the time as he held Leah and stared at the fire. He longed to feel whole again, to be loved, and to experience the emotional satisfaction and fulfillment he'd once known with her. All his dreams and fantasies during the last six years had hinged on the possibility of a life with Leah and their son at some point in the future, but the future had arrived, and he saw it for what it was—a bleak landscape littered with broken dreams and shattered fantasies.

As Leah curled into him and sleepily nuzzled the side of his neck, Brett fought the temptation to abandon his conscience and simply take her into his bed. Starved for one last taste of her passion, he silently cursed the gnawing weakness within himself that prompted such selfish thoughts, and he forced himself to reaffirm his commitment to guiding her through her present crisis.

Brett exhaled raggedly, his thoughts shifting for a moment to the weariness he felt at the prospect of returning to the never-ending battle that he and Micah, and men like them, waged around the globe. In danger of losing his edge and his soul if he remained much longer in the hunt, he realized that his days as a hunter were nearly over. He'd seen too many good men die, and he'd lost everything he valued, but he knew he couldn't walk away until the terrorists who'd placed Leah and their child in jeopardy were all imprisoned.

Brett carried Leah to her bed shortly before dawn, removed her slacks and blouse, and tucked her beneath a down comforter. Placing his weapon on the night table that separated their beds, he discarded all his clothing except his trousers before he stretched out atop his own bed. He wedged a pillow beneath his head, staring absently at the tongues of flame that danced across the top of the logs in the fireplace and listening to the sound of the rain as it pummeled the rooftop above his head.

Brett didn't expect to fall asleep, but his fatigue eventually claimed him and he drifted off, still sick at heart as he anticipated Leah's reaction to him when she recalled their tumultuous past relationship and to the explanation he would have to provide about the threat to her and their son by his enemies.

Eight

Trapped by her panic, Leah screamed. She fought the hands restraining her until the pain deep in her stomach destroyed her dwindling strength and sent her tumbling into the arms of agony. She screamed yet again, a hoarse cry that sounded as though it had been wrenched from the depths of her soul.

A voice she didn't recognize yelled, "Quit fighting me, Leah. You're close. Very close. Give me one more push. Just one more."

"Can't," she muttered between sobs. "Can't push."

Strong hands seized her, shoved her upright, and held her still. Her head rolled forward, long, matted strands of golden hair spilling across her tear-stained, perspiration-drenched face. She groaned weakly, protesting as best she could despite the cramp gripping her mid-section.

"Come on, Leah. One more time for Micah. Just one more for me, and then it'll be all over."

She flailed against his hold, but he brushed her hands aside. "One more," she whispered to herself, knowing that she had no strength left. "One more."

"That's right, little sister. One more time. You can do it. I know you can."

She whimpered a feeble protest and then screamed as the pain exploded inside her again. Someone cursed, the sound vicious as it rang in her ears. She pushed, too frightened now not to. Voices all around her kept yelling at her, insisting that she push. Desperate enough to do anything to end the pain, and despite her certainty that she was on the verge of death, she kept trying to do what they wanted.

"Leah! Wake up!"

Someone shook her, in the same way that a frustrated child shakes a rag doll when it won't talk back. She gasped, grabbing her middle as the muscles there rippled in protest.

"Can't. Can't," she wept, tears streaming down her cheeks. She felt strong hands jerk her forward. She slammed into a hard wall of muscle. Disoriented, she stiffened, opened her eyes, and looked blankly at the fierce expression on the face of the man holding her. "Is he alive? Tell me," she begged, perspiration dripping into her eyes and stinging them. "Is he alive?"

"Leah, wake up. You aren't making any sense."

She clutched at Brett, her fingers sinking into the dark hair that covered his chest. She didn't notice that he flinched as her nails scored his skin. "Is he all right?"

He tugged her close, his confusion evident as he stroked her shaking body and tried to calm her. "Is who all right?"

"The . . ." Uncertain and bewildered, she eased back and studied his features. She saw his concern and what she thought might be a hint of fear. What could he be afraid of? she wondered.

Reaching up, she traced the width of his mouth with her fingertips. He froze, staring at her. She frowned, wondering why he kept looking at her in such an odd way. What was there between them that caused him such anxiety?

She tilted her head to one side, studying him with the open curiosity usually reserved for children when they discovered something new and interesting. She slid her fingertips up the side of his face and into the shaggy dark hair that crowned his head and trailed down his neck. After letting the coarse dark silk slide through her fingers, Leah flexed them and then pressed the pads of each finger against the warmth of his scalp.

Brett shuddered under her touch. His hands tightened, his fingers digging into her waist. She felt pleasure spark to life deep inside her, a ready replacement for the quickly fading memory of pain she'd brought with her from her dream.

"Where are we?" she absently asked as she scanned his harshly carved features yet again. "You look worried. Why?"

Brett frowned. "The Oregon coast. We're in a room at the Seaside Lodge, and I *am* worried."

She shook her head. "No. We can't be. The hospital . . ." Confused, she let her voice trail off. Shoving her tangled hair out of her face, she exhaled and sagged forward against him. Sanity started to pierce her befuddled mind. The dream receded a little more, the edges growing fuzzy. Leah swallowed against the dry, cottony feeling in her throat and mouth. "Water, please."

Brett kept one arm around her, pushed his holstered gun out of the way, and reached for the carafe on the bedside table. After half filling a glass with water, he helped her tilt it to her lips. She drank greedily.

"I had a dream," she whispered once he set aside the glass and drew her back into his arms.

"It sounded more like a nightmare."

"I don't understand."

"You were screaming. I couldn't make out the words, but you sounded terrified and angry."

She felt engulfed by his embrace. He made her feel safe and protected. Why couldn't he love her too? she wondered drowsily.

"I couldn't get you to wake up. You scared the living hell out of me."

She shook her head before she pressed her lips against his shoulder. "Sorry. The dream seemed so real. I think I was having a baby, but no one would tell me if he was all right. Micah was there with me."

"You had a baby in your nightmare?" he asked grimly.

"Sounds crazy, doesn't it?" She hesitated and then admitted, "It hurt. People kept yelling at me to push, but I didn't have any strength left. No one would listen to me, though."

"I would have listened," he insisted, his voice sounding tortured, his eyes filled with pain as he looked down at her. "I would have been there for you if I'd known you needed me."

Startled by his reaction, she said, "Don't be sad, Brett. I'm all right. It was just a dream. I've almost forgotten it."

She snuggled closer, her lips brushing against his bare shoulder yet again, her hands skimming up and down his spine, the muscles rippling beneath her fingertips. She felt him tremble before he tightened his embrace. Leah shifted against him, her insides already throbbing and quaking with need. She sighed.

The sound of her sigh was softer than a gentle breeze on a warm spring day, but Brett still heard it. He forced their bodies apart, gripped her upper arms, and peered down at her face. "What's wrong?"

"Nothing. I'm just . . ."

He slid his hands up to her shoulders, curving his fingers over the slender width. "Your skin's on fire."

"All of me's on fire. I get that way whenever you touch me."

"Leah . . ."

She heard the start of a warning. "No, don't say it, and don't push me away again, Brett. I want you." She saw disbelief and shock reflected in his dark eyes. She stopped him from speaking by placing her fingertips against his lips. "Please don't say no to me again."

He didn't. He muttered a curse, but she heard no anger in the word. Instead, the hard word seemed to echo with the sound of reluctant capitulation.

"Love me, Brett, if only for tonight. Please love me," she whispered against his mouth before quickly sucking his lower lip between her teeth and bathing it with the tip of her tongue.

He groaned into her mouth as their lips mated. He traced the seam of her lips until they parted and then the even line of her teeth, his hunger for her revealed even before he thrust his tongue into her mouth. He explored her thoroughly with deep, hard kisses, and then he proceeded to consume her with an intimate greed that stunned and thrilled her.

Leah opened to him completely, willing to relinquish control, willing to be anything he desired. Too eager, too starved for the taste of him to care who dominated their intimacy, she savored his possession and delighted in the skillful way he ate at her lips and the dark heat within her mouth.

Eager to be free of any barriers between them, she released the catch of her bra, shrugged free of it, and tossed it aside. She pressed her aching breasts against his chest, inhaling the tortured sound Brett made as they shared the purest sensory pleasure, exhaling the answering echo of her utter relief.

She felt his hands urging her even closer. She became pliant, eagerly accommodating his simplest touch. His tongue ravaged the hills and hollows beyond her teeth. She responded in kind, taking her fill of his unique taste and stabbing teasingly at the interior of his mouth until he captured the tip of her tongue with his teeth. She welcomed her captivity as she absorbed the frantic pace of his heartbeat and the heat of his skin as it burned her breasts, and she finally understood that she was experiencing the truth of his hunger for her.

Leah twisted in his arms, her nipples tingling and stiffening as she shifted back and forth across the pelt of dark hair that covered his chest and stomach. She felt herself melting inside, felt herself turning into a seething mass of need that knew no beginning and desired no ending to the glory she found in his arms.

He whispered her name, worshipping her with his low, rough voice even as he left a trail of burning blessings across her body with his tantalizing fingers. Brett suddenly filled his hands with her breasts, molding his fingers over her and measuring the fullness and weight of her warm flesh.

Her breath caught, suspended in her throat until she gasped for air. She felt the tremors that made his fingers tighten over her flesh, and she whimpered her pleasure into his mouth. Relief submerged her at his possessive touch, bringing with it overwhelming emotions and tears that blinded her. A strangled sound escaped her as she choked back her tears. He drank in the salt-tinged sound even as he settled her back against the pillows with gentle hands and a tender look in his troubled eyes.

She reached for him, frantic at the thought of being deprived of the taste and feel of him. She skimmed her fingertips across his chest, branding him with her touch, lightly scoring the flat nipples hidden in his chest hair. His powerful body shuddered. Leah sensed his struggle for self-control, and she felt compelled to make it snap once and for all. She knew she needed to prove to him that they were right for each other.

He seized her hands, pressing hot kisses into her palms before pushing them aside. Sprawled on her back, her long hair a cloud of golden silk around her face and across her shoulders, she trembled with need as her legs shifted restlessly and her hips undulated beneath the hand that stroked her abdomen and upper thighs. Her legs separated of their own accord, her desire for him clearly visible in the stark hunger etched into her features.

Smiling at her, Brett leaned down and wet her lips with the trailing tip of his tongue. She shivered, her love for him a consuming thing. She whispered a prayer that he grasped the powerful feelings he stirred within her.

Running his fingertips from the delicate pulse in the hollow at her throat, down across her swollen breasts and tautly peaked coral nipples, and then on to the soft curves of her belly, he simultaneously soothed and aroused. "Relax, Leah. Let me love you."

She nodded, her lower lip caught between her teeth, her breathing ragged, and her aquamarine eyes glittering with desire. She held her breath, waiting, wondering what he intended. Watching him, she couldn't imagine sharing this kind of intimacy with any other man. She couldn't imagine ever wanting another man at all.

Brett was, she realized in a flash of lucidity, the perfect mate for her heart. She despaired that he might never realize it, and she silently vowed that she would find a way to persuade him that they belonged together.

Bending over her, he cupped her breasts in his hands. He leaned down, took one of her nipples into his mouth, and tenderly nipped at it with his teeth. Air gushed out of her as Leah arched into his mouth, wanting more, wanting anything and everything he felt inclined to give as the tension inside her steadily mounted.

He moved back and forth between her breasts, feeding on her like a starving man as he suckled. She lost track of time, and she lost interest in anything but Brett as he relentlessly stoked the flames of her desire into a raging inferno. She felt the threat of incineration. She even welcomed it.

Gripping his shoulders as he crouched over her, she moaned her pleasure, her nerve endings almost too sensitive to tolerate. Heat and need coiled even more tightly in the lower regions of her body. Her heart raced. She breathed quickly, shallowly, his name spilling repeatedly from her lips. She shifted, restless beneath his hands, growing mindless in her quest for release.

Brett slid his fingers beneath the lace edge of her bikini panties, delving suddenly, deeply into her wet heat with two fingers. Her hips came up off the bed, her cry of pleasure raw as her body adjusted to his forceful intrusion. Her flesh quivered and wept in response, drenching him with her essence.

Quickly stripping the scrap of lace from her hips, Brett moved lower, separated her thighs, and lifted her aching flesh to his mouth. Imprisoning her with his strong hands, he held her still as he explored the soft, damp folds and taut nub secreted behind the golden silk that shielded her delicate feminine secrets.

Tension vibrated through her entire body. She cried out, convinced that she'd been hurled into the center of an inferno. Her hips bucked beneath his skillful tongue and lips. She died a little, a glorious death each time his fingers dipped into the hot, wet recesses of her body, and each time his tongue circled and then stroked the swollen nub that had become so acutely sensitive.

With the pressure inside her threatening to reach flashpoint in a matter of seconds, Leah gasped, "I want you. Please come inside me."

Brett paused, sucked in enough air to fill his lungs, and then he simply intensified his efforts. His tongue swept back and forth across her tender flesh at an increased pace. He carefully introduced three long, narrow fingers into the snug, damp depths of her body.

The combined impact sent charged currents into every part of Leah's trembling body. Feeling electrified by the sensations suffusing her body, she gripped the bedding beneath her hands, her back and legs stiffening with tension. She fought Brett, instinct and need prompting her to try to slow him down. She wanted him inside her. She wanted to feel his strength and love him with her entire being, not just be loved by him.

He thrust his fingers even deeper. Leah resisted

the compelling power of his touch, trying to wrench free of him, her teeth gritted and her head thrown back, but wave after wave of splintering ecstasy threatened to overtake her. His single-minded determination seemed to mock her. Her strength steadily waning, she felt it the instant she began to lose her battle for the climax she wanted to experience with him once their bodies were joined.

"Let go, Leah. Don't fight me. Don't fight your feelings," he urged, his voice gritty and intense. "You need this, so let yourself go. Let me love you."

"No!" she cried even as his words defeated her and triggered her response. "Not yet!"

Leah felt her release detonate with violence and without warning, contracting deep inside her body, sweeping her up, tearing her apart, and then catapulting her into a star-studded heaven of sensory wonder. She called out his name until she grew hoarse. Tears crept from her closed eyes as a firestorm blazed through her senses.

Burning with his own need, Brett held Leah throughout her shattering journey. Despite the cost to himself, he denied his emotions and his body the ultimate joy he knew he would find in Leah's most intimate embrace. He snugged his arms around her hips and pressed his cheek to her pelvis, holding on to her with every bit of his strength. He absorbed the stunning burst of her climax and the powerful aftershocks that quivered through her, and he listened to the broken sound of the sobbing breaths she took.

His heart thundered in his chest as he fought for the control he needed not to take Leah and plunge into her sweet, hot depths. His loins, still pulsing with need, felt on the verge of exploding, and surging rivers of molten desire seared his veins. Brett exhaled raggedly, summoned his strength, forced himself up to a position at her side, and gently gathered her against him. He felt profound relief that Leah came willingly into his arms, but he silently cursed himself for making her weep, because he knew her tears had been born of her frustration with his denial of his own need.

He didn't blame her for her last-minute struggle against him. She'd wanted their bodies joined for a shared climax. He craved the same, just as he craved a life with her, his thoughts and senses focused even now on what it would have been like to be sheathed by her wet heat, her arms holding him, and her legs circling his hips as they shared the same breath with open-mouthed kisses that never ended.

Brett shuddered, his fantasies about making love with Leah torturing him. His flesh felt on the brink of bursting. He trembled beneath her fingers as they combed through the dense pelt that covered his chest.

She tugged free of his grasp when he tried to still her hand. Her fingertips drifted down his body. He held his breath, certain of her intent and helpless to stop her. He needed her touch, knew he would die for it.

His nerves tightened when she curved her hand over his throbbing maleness and cupped his erection. The air in his lungs stilled. Although still attired in his trousers and briefs, his clothing provided little protection against the arousal that streaked fire through his body.

"Why?" she whispered, the word filled with disappointment and tinged with her fatigue. She stroked him, her fingertips skimming up and down the taut length of flesh until he thought he might go insane from wanting her. "Why, Brett?"

He jerked beneath her evocative touch, his loins

filling with an ache that only she could ease. Trying to find a way to answer her question, Brett discovered that his conscience and integrity offered neither solace nor help.

"I can feel how much you want me." She lifted her head, peering up at him so that he could see her confusion and disappointment.

He took her hand and raised it to his lips. Pressing a kiss into her palm, he admitted in a strained voice, "I do want you, more than anything in the world, but you deserve to be protected."

She looked blankly at him for a long moment, but understanding soon filled her face. "Oh, I didn't think about that." She sighed tiredly, tucked her head beneath his chin, and closed her eyes. "We'll stop at a store tomorrow, then."

It was his responsibility to think for both of them, he knew, especially at times like these. He exhaled raggedly as he held her, aware that he could correct her misinterpretation if he wanted to, but he didn't.

He didn't tell her that he had condoms or that he would have used them to protect her, because he never intended for her to face another unplanned pregnancy on her own. With or without her understanding, he intended to protect her from his desire.

Brett chalked up yet another lie to his already tattered conscience, leaned back, and closed his eyes. With Leah cradled against his body, he told himself yet again that he was content simply to care for her when she was vulnerable, but his body and the desire still raging through it made a liar out of him.

Watching over Leah as she slept, he eventually left her bed shortly after dawn to shower, shave, and dress in warm clothing suitable for the inclement weather still buffeting the Pacific Northwest coast-line.

Pausing beside Leah's bed a little while later, Brett placed a note on the night table so that she wouldn't be alarmed if she awoke during his absence. His fingers shook as he nudged aside the thick strands of golden hair that had fallen across her cheek. He froze when she turned her face into his touch. Sighing softly in her sleep, her warm breath washed across his fingertips and palm. Forcing himself to withdraw his hand, he covered her exposed shoulders with the edge of the comforter.

Retrieving his weapon, he exited their room, locking the door securely behind him as he glanced around to make certain that no one observed his movements. He forced his thoughts from Leah to the day ahead. Brett conducted a thorough inspection of the lodge's oceanfront property before making his decision that they would linger for another night at the Seaside Lodge.

He found no sign of the pickup truck that had followed them the previous day, nor did he see any hint of surveillance being conducted. After stopping in the restaurant for a cup of coffee, he persuaded the lodge's owner to open the gift shop earlier than usual.

Certain that Leah would resent being confined in their room, despite the cold temperatures and driz-zly rain, Brett purchased warm, waterproof down jackets and knit caps. He intended to use the weather as an excuse for donning the heavy outer-wear, although his true motive was to shield Leah's distinctive hair from further notice. After calling Washington for an update and learning of Micah's progress in the capture of several more members of the targeted terrorist faction, he ordered a picnic brunch basket and requested that it be delivered by room service.

Brett heard the shower running when he returned to their room. He set aside his purchases, added logs to the low fire still burning in the fireplace, and opened one of the containers of coffee he'd brought back to the room.

Standing in front of the fireplace, his expression reflective, he watched the jets of flame begin to consume the newly placed logs as he recalled the stunning volatility of Leah's passion. He shuddered, his eyes falling closed and his body re-igniting with unresolved hunger for her.

A short while later he looked up from the blazing logs to see Leah emerge from the bathroom. Clad in casual attire and with her hair wrapped in a towel, she smiled shyly and accepted the coffee Brett handed her.

She took a sip of the steaming liquid, her smile widening when she tasted the honey he'd used to sweeten it. "Thanks. You read my mind."

Battling his desire for her, Brett gave her a lazy salute and then settled into the loveseat in front of the fireplace to drink his coffee. Leah took a seat at the edge of the hearth, set aside her coffee, and tugged free the towel that covered her head.

Studying Brett as she ran a brush through her wet hair, she let her gaze travel leisurely from his face to his broad shoulders and then down his flat stomach. Her eyes skipped lower to his muscled long legs and the snug fit of his jeans across the cradle of his narrow hips.

Heat suffused her body, her blood racing through her veins. She'd wanted him, she recalled, with almost frantic desperation the previous night. She still did. The depth of her desire for him continued to startle her, as did her memory of their incomplete lovemaking.

As she'd showered and washed her hair, she'd even wondered if he'd been truthful with her about his inability to protect her. She'd discovered no evidence in her overnight bag to indicate that she owned any birth control measures. Didn't she care enough to protect herself? she wondered. Or had she forsaken intimacy with any and all men? What had happened to her to make her feel that way?

Doubt and confusion still nagged at her, although she didn't know exactly why. She wouldn't know, she realized, until her memories were completely restored. The latest of her returning memories assured her that Brett had not been honest with her about their shared past.

Leah hated finding fault with him, especially now that she'd been the recipient of his sensual generosity. She tingled all over at the thought of the almost excruciating pleasure he'd given her, and the knowledgeable and skillful way in which he'd driven her to a release that had sapped her strength and boggled her mind.

She felt certain that no other man had ever made love to her with such fervent devotion to her pleasure. When she added that fact to her memory that they'd been lovers many years ago, she found it perplexing that he'd denied an intimate relationship between them.

She started when he sat down beside her and took her hairbrush from her, but she didn't resist when he began to brush her hair with long, scalp-tingling strokes. She sat there, warmed by the fire, delighted by his gentleness, aroused by his touch, and fighting the hunger that urged her to turn into his embrace and return the pleasure he'd given her the previous night.

"Couldn't you sleep, or did you think I'd take advantage of you if I found you in my bed this morning?" she asked more bluntly than she intended.

Brett paused, set aside the brush, and ran his fingers through her damp hair. It trickled through his fingers like warm silk. "I needed to run a few errands."

Leah turned and looked at him with troubled eyes. "Are you sure you weren't running away from me?"

Brett frowned and returned her hairbrush, his hands closing into fists as he lowered them to his sides. "That's not something I'd do."

"I'm not sure I believe you."

He got to his feet and crossed the room. Removing the jackets and knit caps he'd purchased from the shopping bag, he glanced in her direction. "How about a walk on the beach?"

"We aren't leaving?"

"We're on vacation, aren't we?" he countered. "I thought we'd stay another day or so, despite the weather."

"We've taken holidays together in the past. Long weekends at a bed-and-breakfast on the Atlantic coast, a ski trip to New England, that sort of thing."

He nodded, caution in his eyes and wariness in the taut lines of his powerful body. He remained on the opposite side of the room.

"We were lovers during my senior year of college, when I lived with Micah in D.C. Why did you deny it?"

"I didn't. That happened a long time ago. You asked if we *are* lovers, present tense."

"You're splitting hairs, Brett, and I don't understand why. Didn't we become lovers again last night?"

"Last night shouldn't have happened. It wasn't fair to you."

"It wasn't fair to *you!*" she exclaimed. Leah left the edge of the hearth. Lifting her hands, she deftly braided her almost-dry hair as she paced in front of the fireplace. She felt Brett's gaze and his tension as he watched her through narrowed eyes, but her own tension was too great for her to feel sympathy for him. "I don't understand how you can say it wasn't fair to me. You made love to me, for heaven's sake. It was . . . I can't even begin to describe how you made me feel."

"Trust me," he suggested bitterly. "It wasn't fair or right."

"You're wrong," she disagreed forcefully, tears stinging her eyes at his denial. "Last night was beautiful. It would've been perfect if you'd let me love you back."

"I was selfish," he gritted out. "I couldn't be near you any longer without touching you and feeling your heat."

"The heat's still inside me, waiting for you, wanting you," she whispered. "I think it always will be. I love . . ."

He abruptly turned away from her, yanking the tags from the jackets before tossing the smaller one on the end of Leah's bed. She approached him and placed her hand on his shoulder. She felt him flinch beneath her fingers, and her heart shattered, but she held her ground, willing to fight for them even if he wouldn't or couldn't.

Brett kept his back to her. "It's cold out. You'll want to bundle up."

"Why are you being so . . ."

He lifted his head, as though scenting the wind like an animal that knows someone or something has violated his territory. Confused by his strange behavior, she fell silent.

"Not now, Leah. Go over by the fireplace." He turned his head and glared down at her when she didn't move. Then he simply waited for her, his eyes hard, his expression settling into implacable lines.

She let her fingers slide free of his shoulder and grudgingly followed his order, despite her resentment that he kept behaving like a sentry at his post. She watched him approach the door, her eyes widening with surprise when he lifted up the back edge of his sweater and rested his fingertips on the gun positioned at the base of his spine. After jerking open the door, he let his hand fall back to his side.

A waitress, her hand raised to knock on the door, stood in the hallway in front of their door. Obviously startled by Brett's scowl, the woman opened her mouth to speak, but she didn't utter a sound. She closed her mouth when Brett handed her several bills, took the picnic basket she held, and thanked her before closing the door in her face.

"Brunch," he announced, his voice like daggers of solid ice. "Why don't we get out of here for a while? I need to stretch my legs and get some fresh air. You do too."

Leah simply stared at him as he placed the basket on a table near the door. He looked at her for several silent seconds and then turned his gaze to the fire. She sensed that he intended to ignore her shock.

Too filled with disbelief to say a word, Leah nodded, tugged the knit cap over her head, and put on the jacket he'd gotten for her. Brett was right about one thing, she realized angrily. She needed to get out of the room. It was too damn small right now for the two of them.

Nine

Withdrawn and silent as they strolled along the beach, Leah reflected on the confusing array of emotions Brett inspired in her heart. She didn't understand his behavior and decided it was time to demand an explanation from him. She also felt increasingly conflicted about the dream she'd had the previous night, especially since certain images had already intruded into her consciousness since she'd wakened that morning.

Although Brett spoke to her several times, Leah ignored him in favor of her thoughts. She barely noticed the gusting coastal winds, the steadily darkening clouds overhead, or the spattering rain.

Pausing at the water's edge after nearly an hour of walking, she stood with her back to Brett. His presence distracted her from the images reasserting themselves in her mind, so she urged, "Go on ahead. I'll catch up."

"I'll be close by if you need me."

"I needed you last night, and I needed you a little while ago," she remarked evenly. "It didn't seem to matter."

She heard a harsh word slip past his lips, but she didn't apologize for criticizing him, nor did she bother to look at him. Instead she assumed that he intended to continue up the beach.

Leah concentrated on the disturbing images that had returned to play through her mind. As in the dream she'd had the night before, she saw herself in a hospital delivery room, people rushing around her, Micah forcing her up when she didn't have the strength to sit up on her own.

And once again she heard a harsh voice shout, "Give me one more push, Leah. One more!"

Something twisted deep inside her body. Placing her hands over her stomach, she stared at the surging, white-capped ocean waves without actually seeing them, her attention focused on the scenes unfolding in her mind.

Leah watched herself, fascinated and stunned by the clarity of her vision. Clad in a hospital gown, drenched in perspiration, and sobbing because she felt so exhausted, she struggled through the final minutes of childbirth. She pushed with what remained of her strength, straining all the while to overcome the pain splintering inside her.

Eventually collapsing against the pillows that Micah had stacked behind her, she grew more and more anxious for the sound of her baby's first cry as the seconds ticked by. Leah sank down to her knees, oblivious of the cold, damp sand, the intensifying force of the rain, and the man who stood several yards behind her in a shallow cave, a picnic basket and folded blanket at his feet, an expression of alarm etched into his hard features as he watched over her.

Leah held her breath for what seemed like forever. She felt the sting of the tears gathering even now in her eyes as she saw herself weep with relief when she finally heard her baby's first outraged wail.

A sob rippled through her as she knelt in the sand. She glimpsed his tiny hands and feet waving in the air as a nurse carried him to her, and she watched herself marveling over him, counting toes and fingers, savoring his warmth, exclaiming over his perfectly shaped head, and soothing his cries of distress. She also heard the rich sound of Micah's laughter, and she noticed the tears that filled her older brother's eyes before he could blink them away.

"I've had a baby," Leah whispered in disbelief. "I have a son."

A strong hand suddenly clamped down on her shoulder. Leah flinched, trying to jerk free, desperate to stay focused on the images in her mind, but they started to fade almost immediately.

"Leah, the tide's starting to come in."

She dodged Brett as he reached for her a second time, arms flailing and fists clenched as she batted his hands away. She blinked and focused inward, determined to see her son's face one more time, but his image faded. She moaned in frustration.

Leah slowly turned her head and peered up at Brett, accusation in her eyes. Reluctantly allowing him to pull her to her feet, she remained subdued as he led her away from the cold ocean froth inching up the beach.

She needed time to think, Leah told herself, time to come to terms with her growing conviction that she was the mother of a small child. Her heart raced with sudden alarm. Where was he? Had he been taken from her? Had he . . . No! She wouldn't let herself imagine the worst.

She scrambled mentally, ransacking her limited memories for some indication of what had happened to her baby son while Brett guided her into a shallow cave that offered protection from the wind and rain. She knew only frustration as she struggled to fill in the gaps surrounding his birth.

Was she fantasizing? she wondered as she absently smoothed away the mixture of raindrops and tears that had wet her face. Had she really delivered a son with Micah's help? She answered her question with an instinct-driven feeling of utter certainty that only a mother could understand.

Brett removed his jacket and dropped it next to the picnic basket, his dark eyes fixed on Leah. His intense emotions showed in his sharp movements as he shook out the blanket and then arranged it on the sandy floor of the cave. "What's going on? You look like you're a million miles away."

Leah finally met his worried gaze. She lifted her chin, the stubbornness that was a part of her personality clearly visible in her expression. "I'm not ready to talk about it yet. I'm still sorting through the details."

"More memories?" he asked, his tone of voice deceptively mild as he studied her pale features.

She nodded, shed her jacket and knit cap, and wandered several feet away to an outcropping of rock shaped like a bench. Sitting down, she massaged her forehead with her fingertips and tried to sort through the tangled web of half memories and dark shadows in her mind. All the while, she kept wondering, *Where is my baby?*

"Leah?"

Startled, she glanced up at Brett, who towered over her. Tears of frustration pooled in her eyes and blurred her vision. She blinked them back, but one slid down her cheek before she could brush it away.

He dropped to his knees in front of her. Curving

his hands over her slender shoulders, he smoothed his open palms up and down her arms. "Talk to me, please."

She shook her head. "I can't. Not yet, anyway."

His expression neutral, Brett carefully drew her forward.

She went willingly, her resistance gone, her emotional strength sapped by her worry and confusion. She needed him too much right now to play games or act coy, but she also needed answers.

"Forgive me for being such a bastard," Brett whispered against her temple as he held her. "It seems as though I'm destined to hurt you every time we're together."

She sagged in his arms, grateful for his presence and no longer furious with herself for loving such an impossibly complex man. She welcomed the emotional strength he always seemed willing to share, just as she appreciated the reassuring power and sturdiness of his body as he held her.

Leah lifted her head to look up at him in exactly the same moment that he peered down at her. Their lips brushed. Eyes widening as they stared at each other, they both froze. They shared the same air, passing it back and forth for almost a full minute before their mouths met and fused.

Leah slipped her arms around his neck, slanted her head to one side, and parted her lips. Brett took her shattered sigh into his mouth.

He eagerly accepted the access she offered, his need of her surpassing his customary restraint. Thrusting his tongue into her mouth, he stroked and tantalized her senses even as he explored the dark warmth and sweetness of her. He kneaded her back with his fingers, then used his palms to leave a sweeping trail of sensation up and down her spine before measuring the narrowness of her waist with his hands.

She tore at his heavy sweater, determined to touch him, to have him naked and inside her before he could think of a reason to deny her the oneness she knew they both craved. His actions matched hers in haste and intensity as he freed her of her sweater and discovered that she wore nothing beneath it. Claiming her mouth again, he molded his hands over her breasts, shuddering as he caressed her.

Her nipples tightened instantly. Her breasts swelled and firmed to fill his hands. She shivered with need too long denied. She clasped his head, cupping the sides of his face as his lips traveled from her mouth to the pulse throbbing in the hollow of her throat and then to the taut coral tips of her breasts.

Her skin sensitive almost beyond bearing, Leah arched into his mouth, gasping as he alternated between her breasts, circling her nipples with his tongue, licking at them and then biting them gently. She felt that she might go mad from the pleasure streaming through her veins and the heat permeating her skin.

"You're on fire for me, aren't you?"

"Yes, yes," she whispered, sounding as feverish as she felt.

Her hands found the fastening of his jeans. He inhaled sharply, shaking beneath her intimate touch when she trailed her fingertips through the coarse nest of hair at the root of his maleness. Brett shuddered, his conscience warring with his need for her.

He straightened, his body filling with increased tension as she explored him. Clenching his teeth, he felt pleasure sear him like a hot brand. Circling his shaft with her fingers, Leah stroked up and down, discovering, measuring, and sighing over the satiny smooth power of his pulsing flesh.

"I want you," he whispered against her lips. He sucked at her lower lip, his teeth and the tip of his tongue tantalizing her while he smoothed his hand across her breasts and plucked at her nipples with his fingertips.

"Then have me," she breathed when he released her mouth. "Have me now."

He cupped her face with shaking hands. "There are things about me you don't remember."

"I know enough," she insisted. "We can talk later."

Thunder rumbled menacingly just beyond the cave's entrance, startling them both. The sky grew darker, diminishing the light in their natural shelter as the rain hammered outside.

Brett froze, self-disgust taunting him. He grabbed Leah's hands, lifted them from his aching flesh, and held them away from his body. He struggled to breathe, to find an island of calm in the center of the storm that was already upon him. His eyes burned like live coals, his face filling with such tension that he looked as though he'd been carved from granite.

"You have to listen to me, Leah."

"Not again," she pleaded. She wilted against him, the air in her lungs gushing out of her, her body weakened by the frustration streaming through it. "Words won't change what I feel."

He molded her to his naked chest. Her nipples pressed into his flesh like tiny daggers, reminding him that this was probably the last time she'd allow him this close.

"Your conscience and your overdeveloped sense of honor are going to be the death of both of us." She exhaled shakily and started over. "Brett, I trust you, I love you, and I want to feel whole again, not like some blasted jigsaw puzzle with half the pieces missing. My feelings for you are all I'm certain of right now. They give you the right to make love to me. *I* give you the right to make love to me. Here. Now." She pressed a tender kiss to his lips. "You keep asking me to trust you, and I do, but you need to trust me now. I know what I want."

He sank down onto his haunches, the muscles in his chest and thighs rippling with strain. She joined him, her breathing still erratic. Positioned knee to knee, they faced each other. Brett dragged his eyes from the sharp rise and fall of her breasts and clenched his fists to keep himself from reaching for her. "I forfeited all my rights where you're concerned a long time ago."

"That's impossible. You said we've been friends for years."

"We were lovers for almost two years. Hell, when we were together, we thought we owned the patent on love, but that was a long time ago. We were engaged to be married. I walked out on you just weeks before the wedding. I told you I didn't love you enough to marry you, even though it was a lie."

"Why?" she asked, shock and confusion in her eyes.

He raked shaking fingers through his dense hair, his hand forming into a fist as he lowered it to his side. "I wanted to protect you. My work with Naval Intelligence was and is dangerous. You would have lived in constant jeopardy as my wife. If my cover had ever been blown, you would have become a pawn in a deadly game where lives are less important than matchsticks. I opted to walk away from you rather than expose you to the risk. I've stayed out of your life for the last six years and three months, despite the cost to both of us."

Leah stared at him when he paused. She felt his eyes search her face, as though seeking some indication that she understood why he'd left her, but she didn't understand at all. She didn't understand anything, it seemed.

"About a week ago one of my European informants alerted me to a contract that had been put out on you and my son. That's why I'm with you. I decided to protect you myself while Micah finishes the final stages of an operation we initiated several years ago in conjunction with Interpol. You didn't just take a fall while you were packing for a vacation trip. Two men were trying to kidnap you. They shoved you to the ground and ran when I showed up."

She swallowed against the dryness in her throat. "The truck in the clinic parking lot. The driver was aiming at us. He wasn't just some drunk who'd lost control."

"They were minions of a terrorist leader who's very close to being taken into custody. Probably the same men who tried to snatch you."

"And the men following us when we left San Francisco?"

"I don't know yet," he admitted. "Washington's checking them out for me."

"Your son. Is he safe?"

Brett nodded, caution filling his gaze. "Matthew's with his grandparents in a safe house. Naval Intelligence supplied a security team at my request."

"You should be with him, not baby-sitting some crazy woman who can't remember most of her life." Leah studied her hands for a moment before hesitantly looking at him. "I have a son too. I just can't remember anything about him. I'm not even sure . . ." Tears flooded her eyes. "I'm not even sure if he's alive. What kind of a mother am I that I can't remember my own child? Do you . . . can you help me find him when—"

Brett seized her hands, jerked her into his lap, and wrapped his arms around her. "Leah, he's fine. He always spends the week before Easter with his grandparents. I wanted you to remember him on your own, not because I force-fed you a bunch of facts about your life that had no real meaning for you."

She felt weak with relief. She stared at him for several seconds, and she suddenly felt as though someone had flipped a switch on in her head as she studied Brett's tense features. Comprehension and hope dawned within her mind in the same moment.

"What are you thinking now?" he asked.

"We had a baby together, didn't we?" she whispered, stunned by the possibility that they'd created a child. "Matthew . . . your Matthew is my son too."

Brett's body ached from the tension suffusing it. "Yes, Matthew is our child. Leah, we haven't seen or spoken to each other in more than six years. I know I hurt you when I broke our engagement. What neither one of us knows is whether or not you've ever forgiven me for abandoning you. You were pregnant with Matthew when I called off the wedding, but you didn't realize it until after you'd quit your job and moved to Monterey. When you discovered your condition, you kept the truth from me. You gave birth to our son without me, and you've raised him alone for almost six years. I didn't find out about him until shortly before his birth. I might never have known about him if it hadn't been for Micah."

Leah heard nothing resembling censure in his voice. She felt compelled to say the words out loud, to clarify her comprehension of Brett's admission one more time. "Matthew is my son, the baby I dreamed about last night. He's *our* baby."

Brett nodded.

"I thought I was going crazy," she confessed, not quite able to grasp everything he'd told her so far. "I kept seeing myself in the delivery room."

"Micah said you had a rough time. I just wish . . ." He sighed. "It doesn't matter now."

"Do you hate me?" Leah asked.

Obviously startled, he didn't say anything at first. "Why would I hate you?"

"I've kept you from your child."

"That's not completely true. I know him from a distance, even though I've never actually met him or spoken to him."

"Through Micah?"

"Yes. He shares your letters, the photographs and home movies you send. He's caught in the middle, Leah. On the one hand, trying to protect you and his godson, and on the other, trying to help me know my son because we're friends and he understood and supported my decision to break our engagement."

Leah frowned, puzzling over an image that popped into her head and then flitted away a few seconds later. "Micah sends me money, doesn't he, even though you said my business was successful."

Brett looked at her with pain-filled eyes. "I want Matthew to have the best. I was afraid you wouldn't take anything from me."

"He needs a father!" she exclaimed. "Not money. Why haven't you forced the issue? Sued for joint custody or just simply demanded to be a part of his life. Am I so hard to deal with, so inflexible that you can't reason with me where our son's welfare is concerned? What kind of a woman am I?"

He clasped her hands and held them tightly. "You're everything a mother should be and more, Leah, so don't doubt yourself because of decisions I made a long time ago. And yes, I want to be a part of Matthew's life, but I didn't want to hurt you again and I don't want my son harmed. I can't be anywhere near the boy until I'm well out of this business. I've tried to keep you both from becoming victims of the violence of my world. I didn't have any other choice. The people I deal with are ruthless, and they don't care who they hurt. Micah and I have always known the risks to our loved ones if our covers are blown and our identities discovered. Placing you, our son, and your family in jeopardy is not at the top of our list of things to do. As careful as we were, though, someone leaked information that resulted in contracts being put out on you and Matthew."

Leah struggled to get free of Brett. "Where is he? I need to see my son. I want my baby!"

He jerked her back into his lap, his grip on her effectively stilling her movement. "Calm down, Leah. You have to believe me when I tell you he's safe. I have no intention of leading professional killers to his doorstep, which is what I might inadvertently do if I take you to him now. The operation is almost over, and I'll be able to get a status report from Micah by tomorrow or the next day. He's running things while I'm with you. Your parents are caring for Matthew, and no one can get to them. No one."

"I don't remember him!" she cried. "I don't remember anything about him."

"You've remembered giving birth to him," he reminded her, "and you'll remember everything else about him, but only if you let it happen naturally."

"I gave him your middle name. Would I have done that if I hated you?" she asked.

"I hope not, but I honestly don't know."

She covered her face with her hands, her thoughts racing a hundred miles a second. She found it next to impossible to deal with everything Brett had just revealed to her. Leah hated all the unanswered questions, just as she resented the confusion that threatened to overwhelm her. She also felt stunned to realize that, regardless of his reasons, she loved a man who'd abandoned her in favor of his professional commitments. And the only reason he was with her now was because she was the mother of his son.

Finally lifting her head, Leah asked, "You really didn't know I was pregnant when you left me?"

"I guess I deserved that," he conceded in a voice tight with control. "No, Leah, I didn't know. I would have found another answer for us if I'd known."

Forgetting the fact that she was only partially dressed, she remained huddled in his lap for a long time, periodically asking questions, lapsing into thoughtful silences, which Brett didn't disturb, and finally falling victim to her emotional and physical fatigue.

He held her pressed to his heart as she dozed in his arms. The rain eventually tapered off, and late morning turned to afternoon. Although muted by both his worry and his determination to protect her, his desire for Leah kept his body aroused and his senses acutely attuned to the vitality and warmth of her skin as he loved her with the reassurance and comfort of his embrace.

Despite his long-held fantasies about a life together, Brett refused to lie to himself about the consequences of revealing the truth about their relationship to Leah. With each passing minute he lost hope that they might find their way back to each other in a lasting and meaningful way.

Ten

Leah spent the next twenty-four hours trying to come to grips with Brett's stunning revelations about their shared past, her escalating worry about the threat to her son by terrorists, and the additional stress of recalling portions of the time she and Brett had spent together in Washington, D.C. In addition, she grappled with the reality that she'd loved him enough to have his child without the benefit of marriage.

She withdrew, emotionally and physically, keeping to her side of the bedroom whenever he was in their room and sitting in front of the fireplace when he left her to her own devices with the cautionary comment that she wasn't to answer the door under any circumstances.

Leah felt grateful that Brett didn't seem inclined to initiate conversation, but she also grew increasingly unsure of herself around him. With her uncertainty came embarrassment that she'd thrown herself at him. Not once, but several times.

She remembered her intense love for him, not just

the highly charged sensuality of the passion they'd shared. Her dreams contained such erotic and arousing images that she frequently wakened during the night to find herself drenched in perspiration and her body tightly coiled with desire that she sensed only Brett could assuage.

As hard as she tried, though, Leah failed to recall any of her emotions during their years apart. Had she continued to love him? Or had she become bitter enough to turn her back on him, thus deliberately depriving Brett of a place in his son's life? If she'd done the latter, Leah wondered how she'd rationalized such behavior in her own mind. No matter how hurt or angry she'd been, she hated the idea that she'd robbed her child of his father.

Mired in her conflicted thoughts, Leah remained silent and aloof even after Brett informed her shortly before dawn the next morning that they needed to move on to another location. She cooperated, dressing and packing hurriedly, willing, despite the strain between them, to defer to his knowledge of the best way to handle the threat posed by the agents of the terrorist faction tracking them.

Brett stopped at yet another rental-car agency to exchange their vehicle for a replacement several hours following their departure from the Seaside Lodge. Leah exited the car, eager for a temporary respite from the boredom of being a passenger and staring at the scenery.

Despite his protest that he didn't want her exposed to any possible danger, she reminded Brett that they were both vulnerable. He persisted in trying to tuck her back into the passenger seat. She grew adamant, refusing to cooperate. "We're in this together, so don't baby me."

Brett clenched his jaws together. Leah watched

emotions flash across his face, feelings that were so diverse, they startled her, but he quickly controlled himself. He jerked a nod in her direction, glanced around the parking lot, visually scanning the area with practiced skill, and then started to step away from her.

Leah stopped him by placing her hand on his arm, her tone subdued when she said, "I just want to stretch my legs. I'll be careful, and I won't wander off. I promise."

He searched her face, worry in his eyes, but he still nodded reluctantly and turned toward the rental-agency clerk, who was headed straight for them. Brett signed the appropriate paperwork and asked the young man to bring the car around. He accepted Leah's help in unloading and then reloading their luggage, but he insisted on handling the heavier pieces.

Although it took her several hours, Leah finally realized that she had to be more patient with herself when dealing with the emotional confusion she felt and the avalanche of memories also tumbling into her mind. The rational side of her personality asserted itself and cautioned that it would take time to sort through all the information her overloaded brain and emotions were trying to process. As a result, she made a concerted effort to relax as the afternoon unfolded.

Leah turned her attention to Brett, who seemed to grow more tense and wary despite the expression of outward calm on his face. She closely watched him as they continued north on less-traveled back roads that led out of Oregon and into rural Washington State. Each time he glanced at her, she got the impression that he was restraining himself by the sheer force of his will.

Restraining himself from doing or saying what? she wondered.

By the time they checked into adjoining rooms at a bed-and-breakfast in rural Washington late in the day, Leah had begun to sense the emotional vulnerability that Brett kept hidden behind an enigmatic mask that he repeatedly donned, a mask that rarely slipped out of place. She suspected that he used it as a tool in his work, not just as a means of protecting his feelings when he feared being hurt or rejected.

Standing in the doorway that separated their bedrooms that evening and watching Brett unpack, Leah remembered his comment about the cost of his lie when he'd told her that he didn't love her enough to marry her. She also recalled his remark that he'd wanted to protect her from the jeopardy of sharing her life with a man who was exposed to constant danger. She didn't doubt either comment, but she saw his withdrawal from her six years ago as a statement that he simply hadn't loved her enough to find a way to make a life together possible.

Leah also began to grasp the emotional isolation inherent in his work, not just his anxiety that he might endanger innocent lives if he allowed himself to have normal relationships. Thanks to her deep feelings for Brett, she knew that love invariably made a person vulnerable. In Brett's case, however, loving anyone carried with it the risk of acts of revenge and death threats from his enemies. The gravity of the burden he carried shook Leah.

She'd become acutely sensitive to his response to her as a woman during their time together, and she still felt bewildered and frustrated by his rejection. She knew he wanted her. She'd felt his desire, and she suspected that his feelings for her went far beyond the physical.

She wondered now if he was denying his desire in order to protect them both from an entanglement that had no future, or if he'd persuaded himself that he was simply protecting her for the sake of their son. Filled with uncertainty, Leah sighed as she leaned against the doorframe, unwittingly drawing Brett's attention.

He looked up from his open suitcase. "Don't you feel well?"

"Your world is a living hell, isn't it?"

He seemed momentarily startled by her question, but he quickly concealed his reaction. "Sometimes," he conceded, surprising her with his candor. "Not always, though."

"I don't know how you cope with the isolation."

He shrugged and glanced down at the sweater he'd pulled out of his luggage. He gave it a blank look before setting it aside. "It's my job, Leah. There are a lot of people like me who work for the government, so I don't consider myself unique." Changing the subject, he asked, "How about some supper? There's a buffet downstairs, or we can ask to have something sent up."

"I'm not hungry."

"Leah, you need to eat."

She shook her head and turned away. She already knew that the kind of nourishment she needed wasn't available to her. She wanted Brett to put his arms around her and hold her. She realized that intimacy with him wouldn't solve the crisis they faced, but she still craved the full force of his passion, and she longed to experience, just for a little while, the sense of completeness she knew she would find in his embrace.

Leah didn't bother to close her bedroom door. She knew Brett would just open it again. As she removed her nightgown from her overnight bag, she wondered if he would ever risk allowing her to breach the walls surrounding his heart.

She gripped her nightgown when she heard his footsteps as he followed her into her room. Her nails dug into the silk fabric until she consciously forced herself to relax.

"I'll have something sent up to the room. Soup and sandwiches, that sort of thing."

Leah's shoulders slumped, but she managed the effort required to cross the room. "Whatever you want."

Brett stood in the open doorway long after she closed the bathroom door and turned on the shower. He finally spoke, his voice rich with despair when he said, "I want *you*, Leah. I want you so badly that my soul aches."

Only half asleep, Brett opened his eyes and reached for his weapon when he heard a floor board creak a few feet from his bed. Poised to roll onto the floor, he froze when he saw Leah step into a puddle of moonlight and then pause. He drew back his arm, his hand clenched into a fist and tension tightening the muscles of his powerful body.

He felt his body begin to heat as he listened to the sound of her shallow breathing. Her anxiety shredded his restraint, and he asked, "Can't you sleep?"

"No."

"He barely heard her for the faintness of her voice. "Would you like to talk?"

"I remember us. I remember the way we were. It's as if I'm standing under a waterfall of memories." Despite the semidarkness of the room, she looked straight at him. She held her hands in front of her,

her fingers tangled together, her body rigid with tension. "Was it so easy to walk away from what we had?"

He swore, the word harsh enough to make Leah flinch. "It was the toughest thing I've ever done, but I know I made the right decision. Unfortunately what I've always feared might happen has happened. You and Matthew are vulnerable because of me." He momentarily wished for a cigarette, a habit he'd given up many years before.

"I want you, Brett."

"Are you sure?" he asked as he pulled himself up against the headboard of the bed, his gaze intent, his senses alert to the slightest hesitation on her part.

"I'm not sure of anything. All I know is that I want a night with you, but I keep wondering if you'll turn away from me again. I need to know the answer, Brett. I need to know if I'm just an obligation, or if you want me as much as I want you."

Too stunned to speak, he simply stared at her. He wondered if she understood what she was saying, what she had just offered him. He felt as though she'd just thrown him a lifeline.

She took a step forward, then paused. "Do you . . . want me?"

He stopped denying himself in that instant. He no longer possessed the fortitude or the strength to be honorable. Lifting the sheet away from his naked body, he shoved it aside. His desire proudly evident, he articulated his need in a voice resonant with the raw emotions coursing through him. "I want you more than I want to breathe, Leah."

Sighing softly, she discarded her nightgown with shaking hands as she walked the final steps to his bed. "Tonight belongs to us. No obligations, no commitments, and no promises to each other that won't be kept. Agreed?"

His heart spasmed with pain, because he felt responsible for her need to qualify the terms under which she was willing to express her desire. Leah paused at the side of the bed, exquisite in her nakedness, but also fragile emotionally. Brett sensed that she wouldn't touch him until he answered her.

"Agreed," he finally said with heartfelt reluctance.

He watched her then through narrowed eyes that had turned black with need, waiting for her to continue at her own pace. Because he understood Leah, he realized that she felt compelled to be totally honest with him. Because he loved her, Brett told himself that he could handle the truth as she viewed it. His conscience called him a liar, but he knew that beggars had little to bargain with, so he said nothing more.

"Tomorrow we'll face reality," she whispered as she knelt at his side and smoothed her fingertips over his sensual lips, his strong chin, and then down across his broad chest. "You'll go back to hunting terrorists and revolutionaries, and I'll return to the task of rebuilding my life, but until then I want to forget that the world even exists."

"It's more than I expected," he admitted, hungry for her, saddened by her need to establish conditions, but realistic enough to accept her terms because he knew he had no other choice. He remained immobile, although his insides burned and throbbed for the intimacy he craved with her, and his hands closed into fists. "Leah, I still love . . ."

She shook her head. Her long golden hair rippled over her shoulders and down her back. "No! Don't tell me you love me. I don't want you to lie, however unintentionally. I just want you to make the world go away for a little while."

She leaned forward, kept him from speaking when she covered his lips with her own, and slowly trailed her fingers through the thick, coarse hair that covered his muscular chest and flat belly. She bathed him with the fire of her desire, her tongue like a darting point of flame as she repeatedly dipped into the wet heat of his mouth while her fingertips danced over his flesh with purposeful intent.

Despite the restraint required, Brett gave her the freedom to explore, to reacquaint herself with a body she had once known almost as well as her own. He gripped the bedding beneath his hands as he savored her intoxicating taste and the feel of her fingertips traveling like hot wands up and down his chest and across his thighs. The muscles of his body bunched and jumped beneath her evocative touch.

Leah sucked his tongue into her mouth and worried the tip of it with her teeth. Brett shuddered, a low groan catching in his throat. He watched her through narrowed eyes when she drew back and peered at him, a funny little smile lifting the edges of her mouth. Shock rocked him when she lifted his hand to her lips and pressed tender kisses to the tip of each finger before scorching his palm with an open-mouthed kiss that sent fire streaking into his soul.

His head fell back and he closed his eyes, shattered by her gentleness, stunned by her sensuality. No woman in his experience had ever loved him with Leah's tender intensity. No woman had ever satisfied his soul *and* his body. No woman but Leah had ever possessed his heart. He knew that no other woman ever would.

She breathed his name as she lifted his other

hand, lingering over his palm, her breath warm, her tongue tantalizingly hot and wet, and her gentleness unbearably sweet. Brett cupped the back of her head, the long strands of her golden mane tangling in his fingers as she bent her head and nuzzled the side of his neck with her lips.

"You're killing me," he muttered.

He felt her smile against the sensitive skin of his throat a heartbeat before she opened her mouth and lapped at the pulse throbbing there. She lifted her head long moments later, her eyes a sultry blue-green, her skin hot to the touch as he cupped her cheek and brought her closer. He felt the press of her taut nipples against his chest in the same instant that she raised her face to his and accepted his hungry, consuming kiss.

Brett absorbed her delicate shiver with his hands when he smoothed them down her arms and urged her even closer. She pressed against him, her high, full breasts plumping sensually against the hard wall of his chest, her nipples stabbing at his hot skin, tormenting him while she parted her lips even more to grant him greater access. He clasped her head with his hands and devoured her lips and mouth, his hunger without boundary, his desire for her escalating as he worshipped her, adored her, and loved her in a silent but eloquent language that only they understood.

She slipped free of him without warning, her soft laughter tempering his disappointment and inciting his imagination even as she moved down his body like a flow of molten gold, pausing here to nuzzle, pausing there to excite, pausing lower still to devastate.

Kneeling between his legs, she watched his face as she slid her hands up and down his powerful thighs, her fingertips veering closer and closer to his jutting maleness with each sweeping movement of her hands. Brett returned her hot gaze, all the while certain that his body would soon ignite from the tension building within him.

Leah softly vowed, "I intend to repay you for the other night."

His eyes shuttered closed. He held as still as he could, but his large body vibrated with barely leashed violence. He groaned, "I may die before you're finished with me."

She suddenly clasped him between her hands, her touch so gloriously bold, so achingly familiar that he had to choke back the emotion brought on by his memories of their shared past. He jerked beneath her fingers, almost not hearing her when she said softly, "I'll make certain you survive the experience."

"Promises, promises," he managed between clenched teeth.

She loved him then, loved him with her deeply sensual nature, her skillful hands, and a cherishing mouth. She loved him until he trembled with the knowledge that he'd die for one last chance to feel the resilient depths of her body closing around him, clasping him, her delicately tremoring inner muscles milking every last drop of passion from him until he collapsed into a mindless heap.

As he savored her devotion, the pressure built inside him to almost unbearable limits. Brett felt a rush of emotion wash over him just before his world suddenly tilted to a dizzying angle. Catapulted into a shimmering cascade of pure sensation, he shuddered violently, his control stretched until it threatened to snap. No longer able to endure her sensual torture, he reared up, seized Leah, and hauled her up the length of his shaking body.

"I wasn't finished," she protested breathlessly as he held her with arms so tightly wrapped around her that she couldn't move.

Brett sucked in enough air to fill his lungs before he raised his head and scowled down at her. "You almost finished me off, and you know it."

She looked at him, smiling like a cat who'd found a full bowl of cream. He swiftly settled her atop his hips, his mouth staking a permanent claim on her lips, his hands possessively closing over her breasts, and his pulsing shaft wedged between their bodies.

Leah gasped, clutching at his shoulders as she shifted experimentally against him. She arched and dipped and stroked, her silk-covered mound like an intimate instrument of mind-shattering pleasure. Brett instantly responded. Lifting his hips, he bucked against her, pledging to give her everything she craved with the movement of his body.

She moaned, whispering, "Now, please. Now," in his ear as she undulated with erotic intent against the hard ridge of flesh trapped beneath her hips.

Brett thought she moved like silk buffeted by a gentle wind. He felt the soft swell of her stomach brushing against his lower abdomen, the dampness of her skin as passion swept through her like a firestorm, and the shivering fullness of her breasts as they nudged against his chest. Gripping her hips, he raised her up so that the tip of his manhood caressed the soft, moist petals of her secret core.

"Welcome me home with your gentle fire, Leah," he begged against her lips as she tried to catch her breath. "I'll die without it."

Positioned on her knees, her gaze melded to his, Leah settled over him in a fluid downward stroke that made them both gasp. She sheathed him completely, taking him deep into the dark heat of her body. Moaning his name, she steadied herself, lifted, dipped, and then rocked her hips in concert with each upward surge of his powerful loins.

Brett felt consumed by a glittering world of pure sensation. The air in his lungs burned, and the muscles in his body thrummed. Hovering at the edge of his pleasure was his certainty that this would be his only night to experience the intensity of Leah's passion. He savored every breathless sound she made and each deliberately provocative movement of her body. Every second they shared became more precious to him than the one before.

He filled his hands with her swollen breasts, molding them, caressing them, and then tugging at her dark coral nipples until they were pebble hard. Ducking his head as she rode him with increasing speed, he took one of the tight peaks into his mouth and sucked strongly.

Leah's head fell back and her eyes drifted closed as she groaned her pleasure. Brett surged up into her body in a relentless counterpoint to the erotic rhythm of her hips. He heard his name spilling from her lips like an incantation, and he felt the subtle change in the lower regions of her body the instant she began to come apart beneath his hands.

She tightened into herself, her breath catching, then streaming out of her body in a rush. She dug her fingers into his shoulders, holding onto him as though he'd become her anchor in a fierce storm. His hands fastened to her hips, he guided her in her breathless pursuit of the summit of her release. And he took into his mouth the sound of her sharp cry as her insides began to spasm and then contract.

He followed after her, his restraint shattering like fine crystal in the aftermath of her turbulent climax as she twisted above him in a final act of giving so pure, so starkly sensual and generously loving that he abandoned himself to the force bursting free of his body.

Bathed in the splintering fire of Leah's love, Brett arched violently, a harsh, guttural cry escaping him as his hips jerked up off the bed. He spent himself in her heat, spasming as he repeatedly thrust upward, finally shuddering as his climax tore through him.

His strength sapped and his emotions vulnerable, he sank back against the headboard. He inhaled Leah's light, sighing kiss as she slid her arms around his neck. Resting her head against his shoulder, she sprawled across him, their bodies still joined and their hearts beating as one.

Unwilling to release her, Brett held her and stroked his hands up and down her back. He listened to her breathing change, felt her bones soften and her limbs grow lax. As she dozed in the security of his embrace, he dreamed of taking her again and again. And in the silence of the midnight hour he whispered of his loneliness and his love for her.

They slept sporadically that night, both eager to indulge needs long denied. They rarely spoke as they feasted on each other, sometimes with explosive haste, always with intense passion, plundering senses and tempting fate as lovers with a complex history have done for centuries.

Eleven

Brett telephoned his superiors at Naval Intelligence while Leah showered and dressed the next morning. Patched through to Europe, he also spoke to Micah, who provided him with a firsthand description of the events that had taken place since their last conversation.

Clad in pale-rose silk slacks and a matching tunic that flowed to her knees, and with her hair fashioned into a loose knot atop her head, Leah walked into his room as he recradled the telephone.

"How goes the battle?" she asked, her heart speeding up as she admired the taut, muscular lines of his naked body.

He smiled, his expression triumphant as he got to his feet. He approached her with the predatory nonchalance of a male animal comfortable with himself and his physical attributes. Having experienced his skillful loving, Leah knew he had every right to his confident manner.

"We've won the war," Brett said. "This one, any-way."

Her eyes skimmed down, then back up his power-ful frame. She inhaled shakily, recalling in vivid detail the erotic night they'd just shared. When she met his gaze, she flushed and worked at getting her senses under control. She said softly, "Then it's finally over."

He nodded, a half smile still tugging at the edges of his sensual mouth. "It appears to be. The terrorist leader we've been hunting for the better part of the last four years is in custody, as are all known members of his faction."

"You must be relieved."

He absently smoothed his hand across her shoul-der, up the side of her neck, and then cupped her cheek. His gaze piercing as he studied her, he ad-mitted, "I'm not sure how I feel. In some respects, it's almost anticlimatic."

Leah flattened her palms against his chest, only half hearing his comments. She absorbed his heat and the steady beat of his heart before leaning forward and pressing kisses to the flat nipples peek-ing through his dense chest hair. Looking up at his strong-boned face a few moments later, she asked, "Do you wish you'd been with Micah instead of baby-sitting me?"

He gathered her into his arms, his nudity allowing her to experience his body's instant reaction to the sumptuous feel of her breasts pressed against his chest and the cradling width of her hips as she swayed against his loins. He lifted her, molding her to him, shifting his narrow hips and rising manhood back and forth before surging against her. He shud-dered and then groaned into her mouth as he kissed her.

Leah clutched at his shoulders, aroused and shaking with renewed desire. "You haven't answered my question," she reminded him a trifle breathlessly once he released her lips.

"I think I just did." He smiled, peering at her through eyes that glowed with unconcealed hunger. "I'm where I want to be, Leah. Haven't you figured that out yet?" Bracing her against him with one strong arm, he raised his wrist and glanced at his watch. "Can you be ready to leave in twenty minutes?"

"Certainly, but what's the rush?"

"You have a date with Matthew."

Open-mouthed with surprise, she watched him stroll naked into the bathroom. The only thing that kept her from following him was the prospect of her reunion with their son.

Despite her determination to remain calm, Leah grew tense as they approached the outskirts of Seattle. Because her memories of her past continued to pour into her consciousness at an almost unmanageable rate of speed, she recognized many of the landmarks she saw.

She also started to recall her final days with Brett and the emotional roller coaster she'd ridden following their breakup. She realized now that her decision to move to Monterey had been born of despair. Her subsequent discovery of her pregnancy had terrified her at first, but Matthew had given her life new meaning and focus. Even though she'd fallen in love with Brett again, she felt anxious about the possibility of being hurt a second time, and she doubted that she could stand losing him twice in her life. Leah also feared subjecting a small child to that kind of emotional turmoil.

"You're awfully quiet," he commented after a lengthy silence.

Leah glanced at him, not surprised by his observation. "I've been thinking about last night."

His eyes traveling from the rearview mirror to the cars in front of them, he asked, "Any regrets?"

She sighed, feeling uncertain but also determined to be honest with him. "No. None at all, as a matter of fact. We'd been building up to it all week."

"And?" he prodded quietly.

"And I'm glad it happened."

"I am too."

"I don't know where we go from here, though," she admitted, hating the awkwardness she felt.

"Last night you didn't want declarations of love or promises that wouldn't be kept. Have you changed your mind, Leah?"

"How do I anticipate or plan for the future if I haven't remembered all of my past?"

"I guess that depends on the person."

"You're a big help," she snapped, her emotions more delicate than she realized.

"You didn't want my help last night. You wanted my body."

Startled by his blunt remark, she really looked at him. She saw his grim facial expression as he watched the road, and she read the tension in the lines of his hard body. Garbed in navy slacks and pullover, he reminded her of a night creature capable of disappearing at will into the darkness. "You make me sound quite calculating."

"That wasn't my intent, but I guess you have every right to be suspicious of my motives." He flicked a glance in her direction. "You've done very well on your own for more than six years. You don't need me or anyone else messing with your emotions or your successful life, do you?"

"I don't know what I need," she confessed. "I'm not

sure of anything right now. It's too soon to make decisions about the future." She hesitated for a moment. "What about Matthew?"

"What about him?" Brett asked tersely.

"You're his father. You have rights."

"Do you intend to grant them, given what you know about me now?"

"You need him as much as he needs you," she said, trying to be fair despite the potential cost to her emotions. "Everything I've learned about you this week assures me that you're an honorable man who has a conscience. On the other side of the coin, I'm remembering pieces of the past, and those memories aren't at all reassuring. You also have a rather risk-filled occupation, but there must be a way to work around it so that Matthew isn't placed in jeopardy again."

"Say that to me once your memory is fully restored. Then I might believe you."

"You sound so cynical. Why are you being like this?"

"I'm being practical, Leah. I don't have any illusions left. I know it's unlikely that there's any room for me in your life. I was a fool to think there might be. But where my son's concerned, I intend to exercise my rights. Once I'm sure I won't jeopardize Matthew's safety, I'll fight you tooth and nail if you deny me a place in his life."

Leah bowed her head and rubbed her temples. She didn't feel prepared to do battle with Brett, nor did she have any desire to be placed in an adversarial position over the welfare of their young son. Too much was at stake, and Matthew didn't deserve to be caught in a tug-of-war between his parents. "Do you think we can have this conversation when I'm capable of holding up my end of it? I'm operating at a slight disadvantage right now."

He gripped the steering wheel, but he didn't force the issue. He simply gave her a hard look as he slowed the car and turned into a long driveway that led to a house set well back from the road.

Leah noticed the name on the mailbox. HOLBROOK. Her heartbeat accelerated. Leaning forward, she studied the sprawling, Tudor-style home and beautifully manicured lawn. Towering Douglas firs lined the drive and bordered either side of the property. Memories that reminded her of splotches of paint on a blank canvas came to life in her mind.

"You grew up here," Brett said as he scanned the grounds for any hint of a threat.

Leah assumed he saw nothing amiss when he proceeded slowly up the driveway. She glanced his way, a hesitant smile on her face. "I recognize the house. There's a row of swings behind the garage, a pool out back that was installed after Dad had his heart attack, and I planted the flowers that line both sides of the front walk the first time I came home to visit after I had Matthew." She frowned. "Is my father in good health?"

He nodded. "Micah and I wanted to make sure he stayed that way, so we had a physician assigned to the security team just in case Martin had any unexpected problems that Helene couldn't handle. It turns out the doctor is an avid fisherman and welcomed a trip to the Pacific Northwest."

"Did he? Have any problems, I mean?" As she spoke, Leah recalled her father's compassion and support when she'd made her decision to have Matthew despite her unmarried state.

"None at all," Brett said as he positioned the car so that he had an advantageous view of the property.

Turning off the ignition, he made no move to exit the vehicle. Instead, he checked his watch and then settled back in his seat. He continued to scan the area visually.

Watching him, Leah realized that his behavior was more a habit than a conscious action on his part. "Are we early?"

"Micah said to expect them just about now."

"What else did Micah say?" she asked in an effort to focus on anything but the nervousness she felt at the prospect of seeing her son.

"The two men who followed us when we left San Francisco were actually police officers on a bona fide vacation." He chuckled ruefully, but his humor quickly faded as he studied a line of fir trees located about fifty yards from their parked car. He frowned and his eyes narrowed when the branches repeatedly stirred.

Leah held her breath as Brett eased his hand to the holstered weapon wedged beneath his thigh and pulled the gun free. He muttered a self-deprecating curse a few seconds later when he noticed two squirrels chasing each other from tree limb to tree limb. She laughed nervously as she watched the cavorting squirrels jump to the ground and dash across the lawn.

A few minutes later they both noticed a late-model station wagon and a dark brown van. The two vehicles moved up the driveway at a sedate pace. The driver of the van flipped his lights on and off, then the driver of the station wagon did the same.

Brett cautioned, "Get down and stay put for a minute," before he exited their rental car, gun in hand as he crouched out of a possible line of fire.

Leah prayed, fervently and silently, that his caution was unnecessary. Still prone on the front seat, she jumped when Brett tugged open the car door a few minutes later. Peering at him, she saw him raise his hand and signal the two vehicles, but she waited for him to motion her up before she lifted her head.

Leah scrambled out of the car, but she hesitated when Brett placed a hand on her arm. "Your parents are up to speed on what's happened, but the boy isn't. We didn't want him frightened."

She searched his face through the tears suddenly blurring her vision. "How do I thank you?" she asked as she gripped his hands.

He looked as though she'd just slapped him. His facade of the competent professional shattered. Leah finally saw the strain in his features and the bleakness of his dark eyes.

Clenching his jaws together, Brett freed himself from her grasp and moved back a step. Fumbling for the aviator-style sunglasses tucked into the breast pocket of his pullover, he put them on.

"Brett . . . "

"You don't have to thank me, damn it," he said in a voice as unyielding as granite. "Just try to forgive me for what I did to us."

"Mom! Hey, Mom! I caught this great fish," Matthew shouted as he barreled out of the station wagon and shot across the lawn.

Torn between Brett's unexpected remark and the voice of her child, Leah said, "Don't disappear before we have a chance to talk."

"I can't stay, Leah. I have to get back to the East Coast. My flight leaves in four hours."

"Hey, Mom! Did you hear me?"

"I'll take you to the airport," she said hurriedly. "Promise me you won't leave on your own."

Brett reluctantly nodded. He yanked his sunglasses off, his gaze sliding from Leah's face to the child bearing down on them. She saw the hunger and pain in Brett's eyes as he studied his son before he grimaced and walked away.

Leah turned and dropped to her knees. Her dark-eyed, dark-haired dynamo of a son raced toward her and then launched himself into her welcoming arms. In that instant she remembered how much and how desperately she loved this innocent child, and she also remembered that he'd helped ease the pain she often felt at living her life without Brett Upton.

"Grandpa cleaned it, and Grammy cooked it for me. Mom! You shoulda been there. It was awesome."

She laughed, hugging him so tightly that he asked, "What's wrong, Mom?"

Her memories of him crashed in around her, making her dizzy and grateful for his very existence. "Nothing, sweetheart. I'm just glad to see you."

"Who's that man?" Matthew asked, his curious gaze on Brett, who stood talking to the men who'd followed Matthew across the lawn.

Leah experienced a moment of panic before her instincts took over. "He's a very dear friend. He works with your Uncle Micah."

"Then he must be a spy too," the little boy said matter-of-factly.

Nonplussed, Leah studied his face. "What do you know about spies?"

"They protect people, but they do it without anyone knowing it."

She smiled to cover her shock. "Who's been telling you about spies?"

"Grandpa Martin, but he said it's a family secret, so I can only talk about it with him and with you."

She drew him close, inhaling his boy smell and hugging him until he squirmed in her arms. "I love you, little man."

He whispered, "I missed you, Mom," before he eased free and wandered in the direction of the man who'd helped create him.

Leah got to her feet and watched her son. She held her breath as Matthew waited with unusual patience for Brett to notice him. She smiled with relief when Brett lowered himself to one knee so that he was at eye level with his son. They both looked solemn as they shook hands.

Leah saw surprise and sudden comprehension in the faces of the men who made up the security team dispatched on Brett's orders as they observed the encounter between their commanding officer and the small boy they'd guarded. The men drifted off in different directions, tactfully allowing father and son the privacy they obviously needed, although they continued to remain alert to any possible threat that might disturb the Holdbrook estate. Her gaze still fixed on Brett and Matthew, Leah felt a burst of optimism spark to life inside her heart.

"They need each other."

She blinked and turned to the man who'd spoken. As she walked into her father's embrace, Leah realized that he'd just verbalized her exact thoughts. "I know, Daddy. I know."

The image of the two of them together—Matthew a miniature version of his father—stayed with her as the day unfolded. The activity level in her parent's home prevented Leah from having a private moment with Brett, who had become the focus of Matthew's attention.

Later that afternoon, Leah drove Brett to the airport. As he paid for his reserved airline ticket and checked his luggage, Leah knew she had to trust her instincts for all their sakes. By the time they reached the departure gate, Brett's flight was in the process of being called.

"I wish you could stay longer."

Appearing surprised by her remark, he cast an exhausted look at her, searching her face as though to confirm her sincerity. "The paperwork that follows an international operation like this takes weeks, sometimes months, to clean up."

"I realize now that you're still on active duty, and I know you have responsibilities." She shoved a tendril of golden hair from her face. "I'm remembering even more now. Seeing Matthew and my parents helped speed up the process."

Brett nodded, shifting restlessly as the line of passengers grew shorter. "You'll be fine."

"Did you really not love me enough to marry me?"

He looked stunned. "I was trying to protect you."

"That's not what I asked."

He took her arm and led her to an alcove a few feet away. "I loved you, Leah, more than I've ever loved anyone in my life."

She inched closer and slipped her arms around his waist. The scent of white ginger drifted up from her skin to tease his senses. Brett gripped her upper arms. Leah shivered beneath his hands, her hunger for him never dormant for long.

"Our son's an incredible little guy, thanks to you."

She peered up at him to see in his dark eyes what could only be described as regret for all that he'd missed during their years apart. Although she felt achingly vulnerable, she also felt oddly strengthened by Brett's admission. "Do you love me at all now?"

"How can you ask such a question?" he demanded, his fatigue showing in his flaring temper.

"I have to ask. I can't guess about something this important."

He wrapped his arms around her, took her mouth, and plundered it until they were both breathless. "I love you more than life itself. I always will."

Her lips tingling and her heart racing, she choked back the tears clogging her throat. "I told you earlier that I think you're an honorable man, but I'm starting to believe that you're an incredibly misguided one too." Despite the current of tension flowing between them, she whispered, "I love you, Brett Matthew Upton. I'm sure now that I've never stopped loving you. And your son will love you when he's given the chance to know you."

Too shocked to speak, Brett stared at her. They both heard a voice announce over a loudspeaker the final boarding call for his flight. Leah clutched the front of his shirt.

"As much as I want to stay, I can't. Leah, I'll call you and we'll talk. You said it yourself this morning. You aren't ready to make important decisions about the future right now. I don't want you to regret—"

"Listen to me, and really hear what I'm about to say to you. I'm not going to change my mind. I want you to come home to us when you're ready. Matthew needs you. He's waited too long to know his father, and I've waited six years to feel whole again. Please don't make us wait much longer. We want you, and we need you. I think you need us too."

"Sir," interrupted the gate agent, "if you're going to board this flight, you'll have to do so now."

He dropped a hard kiss on her lips, then promised, "I'll call you as soon as I can."

Leah hurried along at his side as he strode down the tunnel that connected the boarding gate to the aircraft. She paused at the door of the plane as Brett's gaze swept hungrily across her face one last time.

"Trust *me* this time, Brett. And try to find a way to trust *us*."

"I want to believe you," he admitted.

"You can," Leah insisted. "You can."

The stark look of longing etched into his face made Leah sag against the wall as she lost sight of Brett. After the door slammed closed, the gate agent, a middle-aged woman with a kind face, touched her arm. "You'll have to return to the main terminal now, miss."

She nodded. Although nearly blinded by her tears, she made the trek back up the hallway, where two members of the security team discreetly walked her the rest of the way out of the terminal and drove her back to her family home. Leah waited then, waited for four of the longest weeks of her life, but Brett never called.

It was Micah, not Brett, who finally summoned her to Washington, D.C., but only after she'd returned to Monterey, accompanied by security-team members, reinstalled Matthew in his preschool class, and listlessly resumed her work in the flower shop. Helene and Martin Holbrook arrived without warning to care for their grandson the night that Micah telephoned. Leah felt like the object of a covert conspiracy by the time she boarded her chartered flight for the trip to the East Coast.

Twelve

Leah flashed a startled glance in Micah's direction when the driver of the car that had collected her at the airport turned into the grounds of Arlington National Cemetery. The uniformed young man guided the car down a series of narrow lanes deep within the confines of the resting-place of several generations of fallen warriors.

Micah shook his head, his eyes darting to the other occupants of the car as though to caution her against speaking. Because she recalled her brother's passion for privacy, Leah remained silent until the other passengers—grim-faced naval officers clad in dress blue uniforms—exited the vehicle once the driver pulled into line behind several other official-looking cars.

She turned again to Micah and noticed his reluctance to return her gaze. He stared, instead, at the mourners gathered less than twenty feet away from their parked car.

"What's going on, Micah?"

He cleared his throat, and he didn't speak right

away. Leah felt a surge of apprehension threaten her emotions, but she told herself that her brother was just being his usual mysterious self.

He pushed open the car door. "Come with me, Leah. I need your help. So does Brett."

She folded her hands in her lap. "I'm not budging from this car until you explain what we're doing here."

"We're attending a funeral."

"All right, big brother, you owe me an explanation, and it had better make sense, because right now I think you've lost your mind."

He gripped her hand. She felt and saw his escalating tension, not just the lines of stress deepening the grooves on either side of his mouth. She got the impression that he was just barely holding onto his emotions.

"Will you trust me and come with me now?" he asked in a low voice.

"I'm a little tired of men asking me to trust them, Micah. Brett asked me to trust him, and I did. That was a mistake I don't intend to make again."

Exhaling harshly, he stabbed her with a look that frightened her. "Commander Brett Matthew Upton has officially been declared killed in the line of duty by the United States Navy. His funeral services are about to begin. Now, will you come with me?"

Leah blanched. Shock ricocheted through her. Micah gripped her shaking hands and hurried her out of the car before she could protest. "Don't hold back your emotions. This is important."

Too stunned to make any sense of his comment, she stumbled to the gravesite with Micah's assistance and sank down onto one of several chairs lined up in front of a flag-draped coffin. Leah listened numbly to the navy chaplain as he spoke in a reserved tone of voice.

"Eulogizing a man cut down in his prime is often a difficult task. In this case, however, it is not. The achievements of Commander Brett Upton are numerous. He served his country with distinction, honoring both his nation and the United States Navy in the performance of his duty. A graduate of the Naval Academy, he began his career with the highest expectations of his commander-in-chief and his superior officers. Not once did he fail to achieve those expectations. If anything, Brett Upton exceeded them, time and time again, and often at great personal risk to himself."

Leah sagged against Micah. He pulled her to her feet a few minutes later, and he slipped his arm around her to steady her once the chaplain completed his remarks. She wept for Brett and all the warmth and love he hadn't had time to experience in his life. She wept for her son, because he would never know his father. And she wept for herself, because she knew she would never love a man as she'd loved Brett.

A captain stepped forward and presented her with the flag after it was removed from the top of the coffin and folded in a poignant ceremony by the attending naval honor guard unit. Crying soundlessly, Leah didn't notice the strained look Micah exchanged with his commanding officer as the two men saluted one another.

She numbly watched mourners, primarily men and women in uniform, walk by the coffin. Each person placed a long-stemmed red rose atop the coffin. No one spoke to Leah, but several people paused to shake Micah's hand and exchange a few words.

Leah fought to resurrect her poise. She felt consumed by a nightmarish sense of loss as Micah guided her to a car other than the one that had brought them to the funeral. "Take it easy, little sister. Everything's going to be fine," he promised as he glanced repeatedly at the rearview mirror. Exiting the cemetery, he remained alert and watchful.

Leah stared blankly at the passing scenery as they traveled the congested roadways that eventually led out of the nation's capital and into a Virginia suburb. Micah finally pulled up a short driveway to a house she didn't recognize. He pressed a button, and the garage door closed behind them.

"Thank God that's over."

"What happened to him?"

"Nothing."

Bewildered, she stared at him.

"We're here. You can go inside now."

"Here where, Micah?" she exclaimed, the strain of the last hours showing. "What are you trying to do to me?"

"Brett's waiting for you."

She rubbed her temples with her free hand as her eyes filled with tears again. "You aren't making any sense."

"The funeral was staged. I had no choice but to put you through that hell. I'm sorry."

She stared at him, unable at first to comprehend what he'd just said. "How could you do that to me? I'm your sister, for God's sake."

"It had to look real. There were people there taking photos of every move we made, every tear you shed."

"Micah!" She shoved the folded flag at him and reached for her purse, intent on calling a cab so that she could escape her brother's lunacy.

He grabbed her and gave her a good shake. "Listen

to me. It was the only way we could think of to make sure he's protected from retribution by the thugs who almost killed you and Matthew."

"They're in jail. You know that."

"They have friends, Leah. Brett brought down one of the most powerful terrorist leaders in the Middle East. He was the lynchpin of the entire operation. The wrong people know it, and they want him dead. I just helped mop up at the end."

Desperate to believe him, she whispered, "Brett's really alive?"

"Yes."

"You should've told me the truth."

He thrust his fingers through his dense golden hair. "You can't fake that kind of soul-deep grief, Leah. You were the key to the authenticity we needed, so I opted to use you."

Stunned, she whispered, "You need a new career, big brother. This one's turned you into a heartless bastard."

Micah Holbrook flinched, but he didn't deny her observation. "I did it because I don't want my best friend assassinated by death merchants from the other side of the world, because Matthew deserves a father, and because I don't want my baby sister heartsick over a man for the rest of her life. I wanted to make sure you three have a chance at a real life together once the dust settles and these people forget about Brett. It'll take time, of course, but—"

"Is he expecting me?" she cut in, too frustrated with his machinations to listen to anything else he had to say.

"Yes, but don't tell him I took you to that funeral without telling you the truth first, or he'll have my head on a platter."

"You'd deserve it," she declared, still raw-nerved from the ordeal she'd just endured.

Micah winced. "I know, but I had to make this thing look real."

"It felt real, Micah, much too real. I love him."

"Tell me something I don't already know." He hugged her and then leaned past her to push open her door. "I'll wait out here for you."

Still feeling more than a little shell-shocked, Leah made her way into the house. She hesitated when she saw a man standing with his back to her in the kitchen. When he turned to look at her, she recognized Brett, despite his short hair, the gray added at his temples, the glasses he wore, and the mustache that now covered his upper lip.

"How was your flight?" he asked.

She opened her mouth, but she just as quickly snapped it shut. She decided that she liked the nervousness she sensed in him. Where was it written? she wondered, that he had the right to be calm when she felt as though she'd been fed through a paper shredder.

"I hope the subterfuge of getting you here wasn't too much of a hassle."

"Why exactly did you have me brought here?" she asked, moving closer and openly studying the cosmetic changes in his appearance. He looked unexpectedly civilized, especially with the upscale wardrobe he obviously now owned. She doubted, though, that the inner man, that overly protective renegade who thought he had all the answers, was situated too far out of reach.

"I'm about to disappear, courtesy of the navy's version of the Witness Protection Program. I don't know how long I'll be gone, but I needed to see you one last time. I wanted to tell you that I love you. I've always loved you. If I had any other choice, I'd cash in my chips and join you in Monterey."

"We aren't invited to your new life?" she asked, referring to herself and Matthew.

He frowned. "This isn't a party, Leah."

She nodded. "You're walking out on me again, aren't you?"

"Not by choice."

She glanced down, ran her fingertips along the edge of the kitchen counter, and then gave him a penetrating look. Deep in her chest, her heart felt like a piece of chipped rock. "You didn't call."

"I couldn't risk it."

"You promised."

He took several steps in her direction. "I know."

"Where will you go?"

"I can't tell you. It's classified."

She laughed, the sound too high-pitched to reflect any real humor. "Any ideas on how I'm supposed to cope with all these changes?"

He moved closer, his hands casually tucked in his trouser pockets, the fabric straining across his loins. Her gaze snapped on the potent reminder of his skill as a lover and the passion they'd shared. She felt her insides start to simmer, and she fought the feeling in favor of keeping her wits in a straight line.

"I didn't want to just disappear without telling you the truth, and I was selfish enough to want to see you one more time. I may be gone for a year or two, perhaps longer." He extended his hand.

She ducked beyond his reach and positioned herself in front of the kitchen window. "Do you have any comprehension of how I felt when I stood at a gravesite and listened to your eulogy? Can you even begin to grasp how devastated I was?"

He grabbed her, trapped her against his chest, and

forced her chin up so that he could see her eyes. "Micah took you there without warning you about what was going to happen, didn't he?"

"He said he needed my reaction to be authentic." Tears filled her eyes as Brett muttered an ugly word. "I thought you were dead." She felt her self-control splinter apart. Tears spilled past her lower lids and streamed down her cheeks. "I thought you were dead," she sobbed.

"My God, Leah, I'm so sorry." He held her as she released the pent-up emotions she'd held at bay for the last four weeks.

She finally looked up at him, her lashes and cheeks still wet. She shuddered as his hands swept up and down her back and then roamed over her hips. In spite of the clothes she wore, he made her feel almost naked as he caressed her.

Brett brought her up and against him, a low moan escaping him as she repeatedly nudged against the ridge of flesh trapped between their lower bodies. Trembling with desire, Leah slid her arms around his waist, her fingers pressing against the base of his spine to bring him even nearer as she fastened her lips to his.

She savored his hot response, drinking it in like a woman parched, even as he fed on her, his tongue stabbing into her mouth as he thrust his hips against the welcome of her cradling thighs. She shivered violently, wanting him with a craving so intense, she couldn't even begin to articulate it. Breathless, she held on to him and lost herself in the sensations rioting through her body. She groaned when Brett lifted his head and dragged in enough air to nourish his lungs.

"Why is it that men are so stupid some of the time?" she asked once she could speak. "They think they can plan every little detail and expect a woman to just go along with them."

"I'll write," he promised, his lips whispering along the side of her neck and driving· her mad with longing.

"That's not good enough," she insisted, her fingers stroking the front of his trousers. She felt the surging power of his body against her hand, and she wanted him buried deep inside her.

"I can't risk calling."

"Then don't." She dragged her hands from him and clenched them into fists to keep from touching him.

Brett lifted his head and peered down at her, uncertainty in his dark eyes, tension of a different kind sifting into him. He edged her back against the kitchen counter with the power of his lower body, trapping her there as he studied her. "What about Matthew?" he finally asked.

"He's my child. I'll worry about him, so don't give my son another thought."

He blinked in surprise, then said in a low voice, "You're furious."

"No kidding!" She glared at him, stunning him with the flashing blue-green of her eyes, stabbing her finger against his chest so many times that she expected to find a dent there if she decided to look beneath the pin-striped shirt and pullover sweater he wore. "You're depriving me, once again, of the right to choose my own destiny. How do you expect me to feel?"

"You have to trust me to know what's best for all of us, Leah."

"No, I don't. You need to trust the strength of our love, as well as our ability to adapt as a family to the situation we're all facing."

"It won't be safe."

"There's danger everywhere," she argued. "But we'll manage."

"I don't have the right to expose you or Matthew to a high-risk situation. There are too many unknown factors. As lonely as I'll be without you, I have to do the right thing for all of us. It's crucial. People want me dead. I don't want the two of you caught in the cross fire."

As agitated as she felt, Leah managed to calm herself. She experienced the dread of impending loss, and she intended to do everything in her power to stop it from happening again. "Your success depends on your ability to blend in and not be noticed. Correct?"

Brett nodded, his expression cautious.

"No one will expect your new identity to include a wife and child."

He looked startled, then wary. "Are you proposing?"

She scowled at him. "One of us needs to, don't you think?"

"Leah, the risks . . ."

". . . do not outweigh the benefits." She grabbed his shoulders. "Don't you get it, Brett? You did this once before. You made a decision without allowing me the right to make an informed choice. I don't need you to think for me. I'm perfectly capable of making my own decisions. I've been doing it for a long time now."

"I don't believe in fairy tales or happily-ever-after endings, Leah. I wasn't kidding before when I told you I'd lost all of my illusions."

Determined to persuade him to see her perspective, Leah reminded him, "You almost destroyed both our lives six years ago by being honorable. Now that I understand your reasoning back then, I can accept what you did, even forgive it, but you can't do the same thing to us again. We're different people this time around, stronger and hopefully wiser. I have rights, and I'm officially exercising them. I love you, and I need to be with you, whatever the circumstances. Our son deserves a loving father, and you deserve to be loved by Matthew. You've lived without us. Now live with us. Love us and let us love you. It's time, Brett. God will not give us a third chance to get it right."

"You're asking me to let you risk two lives."

"I'm asking you to risk your emotions and think with your heart where we're concerned. We can be smart about everything else, but we'll do it together."

"There will be sacrifices. You won't be able to see your family for a long time," he warned.

"They'll understand. Micah will help them through the tough times."

"We can't go back to Monterey."

"I'll adjust. So will Sarah. She can buy me out of the business whenever she's ready. You're more important than a place. *We're* more important than a place."

Brett took her hands and brought them to his lips. Sucking the tips of her fingers into his mouth, he laved them with his tongue and sent bursts of sensations into her nerves. "I love you so much, Leah. The thought of not seeing you for a year or two, or even three, leaves me cold inside."

She smiled, a scintilating little smile. "I told you my heat is yours whenever you want it."

"Now?" he asked as he wrapped his arms around her.

"Forever."

He took her mouth, and he forgot about the chaos

taking place in various parts of the world and about his future brother-in-law, who was still cooling his heels in the garage.

Much, much later, Leah said, "I wonder what I'll look like as a redhead."

Sprawled atop her, Brett shifted his hips in a teasing motion that made her moan. "I think we're about to find out," he commented before delving deeply into the heat she very eagerly shared.

THE EDITOR'S CORNER

Next month LOVESWEPT presents an Easter parade of six fabulous romances. Not even April showers can douse the terrific mood you'll be in after reading each and every one of these treasures.

The hero of Susan Connell's new LOVESWEPT, #606, is truly **SOME KIND OF WONDERFUL.** As mysterious and exciting as the Greek islands he calls home, Alex Stoner is like a gorgeous god whose mouth promises pagan pleasures. He's also a cool businessman who never lets a woman get close. But prim and proper Sandy Patterson, widow of his college roommate, is unlike any he's ever known, and he sets out to make her ache for his own brand of passion. Susan takes you on a roller coaster of emotion with this romance.

Kay Hooper continues her MEN OF MYSTERIES PAST series with **HUNTING THE WOLFE,** LOVESWEPT #607. Security expert Wolfe Nickerson appeared in the first book in the series, **THE TOUCH OF MAX,** LOVESWEPT #595, and in this new novel, he almost finds himself bested by a pint-sized computer programmer. Storm Tremaine blows into his life like a force of nature, promising him the chase of his life . . . and hinting she's fast enough to catch him! When he surrenders to her womanly charms, he doesn't know that Storm holds a secret . . . a secret that could forever destroy his trust. Kay is at her best with this terrific love story.

BREATHLESS, LOVESWEPT #608 by Diane Pershing, is how Hollis Blake feels when Tony Stellini walks into her gift shop. The tall, dark, and sensuous lawyer makes the air sizzle with his wildfire energy, and for the first time Hollis longs to taste every pleasure she's never had, pursue all the dreams she's been denied. Her innocence stirs an overpowering desire in Tony, but he senses that with this untouched beauty, he has to take it one slow, delicious step at a time. This is a romance to relish, a treat from Diane.

Linda Cajio begins **DANCING IN THE DARK,** LOVESWEPT #609, with an eye-opening scene in which the hero is engaged in a sacred ceremony and dancing naked in the woods! Jake Halford feels a little silly performing the men's movement ritual, but Charity Brown feels downright embarrassed at catching him at it. How can she ever work with her company's new vice president without remembering the thrilling sight of his muscles and power? The way Linda has these two learning how to mix business and pleasure is a pure delight.

HANNAH'S HUNK, LOVESWEPT #610 by Sandra Chastain, is nothing less than a sexy rebel with a southern drawl . . . and an ex-con whom Hannah Clendening "kidnaps" so he could pose for the cover of her Fantasy Romance. Dan Bailey agrees, but only if Hannah plays the heroine and he gets to kiss her. When desire flares between them like a force field, neither believes that what they feel could last. Of course Sandra, with her usual wit and charm, makes sure there's a happily ever after for this unusual couple.

Finally, there's **THE TROUBLE WITH MAGIC,** LOVESWEPT #611 by Mary Kay McComas. Harriet Wheaton has an outrageous plan to keep Payton Dunsmore from foreclosing on the great manor house on Jovette Island. Marooning them there, she tells him that she's trying to fulfill the old legend of enemies meeting on Jovette and falling in love! Payton's furious at first, but he soon succumbs to the enchantment of the island . . . and Harriet herself. Mary Kay delivers pure magic with this marvelous romance.

On sale this month from FANFARE are four outstanding novels. If you missed **TEMPERATURES RISING** by blockbuster author Sandra Brown when it first came out, now's your chance to grab a copy of this wonderfully evocative love story. Chantal duPont tells herself that she needs Scout Ritland only to build a much-needed bridge on the South Pacific island she calls home. And when the time comes for him to leave, she must make the painful decision of letting him go—or risking everything by taking a chance on love.

From beloved author Rosanne Bittner comes **OUTLAW HEARTS,** a stirring new novel of heart-stopping danger and burning desire. At twenty, Miranda Hayes has known more than her share of heartache and loss. Then she clashes with the notorious gunslinger Jake Harkner, a hard-hearted loner with a price on his head, and finds within herself a deep well of courage . . . and feelings of desire she's never known before.

Fanfare is proud to publish **THE LAST HIGHWAYMAN,** the first historical romance by Katherine O'Neal, a truly exciting new voice in women's fiction. In this delectable action-packed novel, Christina has money, power, and position, but she has never known reckless passion, never found enduring love . . . until she is kidnapped by a dangerously handsome bandit who needs her to heal his tormented soul.

In the bestselling tradition of Danielle Steel, **CONFI-DENCES** by Penny Hayden is a warm, deeply moving novel about four "thirty-something" mothers whose lives are interwoven by a long-held secret—a secret that could now save the life of a seventeen-year-old boy dying of leukemia.

Also available now in the hardcover edition from Double-day is **MASK OF NIGHT** by Lois Wolfe, a stunning historical novel of romantic suspense. When an actress and a cattle rancher join forces against a diabolical villain, the result is an unforgettable story of love and vengeance.

Happy reading!

With warmest wishes,

Nita Taublib

Nita Taublib
Associate Publisher
LOVESWEPT and FANFARE

Don't miss these fabulous
Bantam
Women's Fiction
titles
on sale in FEBRUARY

TEMPERATURES RISING
by Sandra Brown

OUTLAW HEARTS
by Rosanne Bittner

THE LAST HIGHWAYMAN
by Katherine O'Neal

CONFIDENCES
by Penny Hayden

In hardcover from Doubleday,
MASK OF NIGHT
by Lois Wolfe
author of THE SCHEMERS

From the *New York Times*
bestselling author of
A Whole New Light and *The Texas! Trilogy*

Sandra Brown
TEMPERATURES RISING

In this wonderfully evocative love story, a man and a woman from vastly different worlds are brought together on a lush South Pacific island.

Chantal duPont loved her tropical island home and would do anything she could to protect it from the greed of outsiders. To her the developers of the new Coral Reef resort were the enemy, plain and simple. So when she devised a plan to save her village, she never expected to come up against a man like Scout Ritland. She told herself that she only needed Scout to build a much-needed bridge for her people. But as the days pass and the work progresses, Chantal has to face the possibility that Scout means more to her than she had thought. And when the time comes for him to leave, she will have to make the painful decision to let him go—or risk everything by taking a chance on love.

OUTLAW HEARTS
by
Rosanne Bittner

**From the author of THUNDER ON THE PLAINS comes
the sweeping, heart-stirring saga of a man who lived by the
gun and the daring young woman who taught him how to
love. . . .**

*At twenty, Miranda Hayes had known more than her share of heartache
and loss. Widowed by the war, orphaned by a vicious band of rebel
raiders, she was a woman alone in a harsh, unyielding frontier. Then she
clashed with the notorious gunslinger Jake Harkner, a hard-hearted loner
with a price on his head, and found within herself a deep well of
courage . . . and feelings of desire she'd never known.*

*Hunted by lawmen and desperadoes alike, haunted by his brutal past,
Jake had spent a lifetime on the dusty trail—and on the run. Until he met
a vibrant, honey-haired beauty who was determined to change his violent
ways, who loved him enough to risk her life to be his woman . . . an
outlaw's woman.*

*From the vast plains of the Midwest across the Oregon Trail to the
sun-drenched valleys of southern California, from the blazing Nevada
desert to the boomtowns of Colorado, Miranda and Jake struggled to
endure amid the perils of a lawless wilderness. In a world of heart-
stopping danger and burning desire, could their hard-won love survive the
shadows that stalked their happiness?*

Jake put his head back again, closing his eyes and listening to
the storm, remembering another storm, one that hit on a night
he would never forget. Should he tell her? He knew she was
wondering, and what better way to make her hate him than to
tell her the truth? The storm only brought it all back more

vividly anyway. Thunder clapped again, and he could hear the gun going off at the same time. He could see the look of astonishment on his father's face.

He waited a moment longer, another crash of thunder making him wince and put a hand to his forehead.

"Jake? What's wrong?"

He ran his hand through his hair. "Where's the whiskey I bought back at that fort?" He saw her hesitate, knew what she was thinking. Giving whiskey to an ailing man was one thing, but it was something completely different when given to a perfectly healthy man with a notorious reputation. "Don't worry. I don't react to whiskey like my pa used to," he told her, "although he didn't need alcohol to bring out the worst in him."

Miranda watched him a moment longer, then nodded toward the pile of blankets. "You're leaning against it—in the crate under those blankets."

Jake turned to search, grinning to himself at the realization she must have put it out of sight in hopes he would forget he had it. He removed a flask from the crate and uncorked it, turning back around and taking a swallow. He let it burn its way down his throat and into his stomach. He seldom drank much, hated the memories of what whiskey did to his father, how mean it made him. Still, right now it gave him the added courage he needed to shock Miranda Hayes out of any feelings she might have for him. He did not need or want to talk about this, but if it would take the light out of Miranda Hayes's eyes when she looked at him, it would be worth the telling.

He lowered the bottle, staring at it for a moment, taking another drag on the cheroot. "I killed him," he told her.

Miranda frowned, taking her gaze from her sewing and meeting his eyes. "Killed whom?"

Jake held her eyes, giving her his darkest, meanest look. "My *pa*! I shot him dead. What do you think of that?" To his frustration and amazement, he saw no shock, no animosity, no horror. He saw only a strange sorrow.

"I know," she answered. "I'm sorry, Jake."

He just stared at her a moment, astounded at her reply, suddenly angry with her. "What the hell do you mean, you *know*! And you're *sorry*? I didn't tell you in order to get your damn *pity*!" He let out a nervous laugh. "Jesus, woman, what the hell is the matter with you?"

Miranda put down the sewing. "You expected me to be surprised? After all, that always has been the rumor. After what you told me back at the cabin, I had no doubt it was true. What I'm sorry about is you must have had a good cause, which means your father must have been doing something terrible to you or to someone you loved. What did he do, Jake? Does it have something to do with Santana?"

He rolled his eyes and took another swallow of whiskey. "You're incredible, you know that? What the hell kind of a man kills his own pa?"

"A desperate one, and I'm betting he wasn't a man at all. He was probably still a boy, and sometimes that same boy comes charging out of the man, fighting, angry, defending himself, refusing to have feelings because he might hurt again, and he doesn't want to hurt. He's afraid—"

"Shut up!" He wanted her to flinch, but she didn't. Damn her! Damn slip of a woman! "Maybe what I ought to do is show you just how much of a man I *really* am!" he deliberately snarled. He turned and crammed the whiskey back into the crate, then dropped the cheroot back into the tin cup. He began unbuckling his gunbelt.

Miranda truly wondered if she had gone too far this time. The man hated it when someone saw through the outer meanness to his vulnerability. It made him furious, and a furious Jake Harkner might not be as safe as she had supposed. Had she trusted too much?

He tossed the gunbelt aside, and before Miranda could react, he lunged at her and grasped her arms tightly, painfully. Her eyes widened, and she dropped her sewing when he lifted and moved her like a ragdoll, pushing her against the blankets which he had himself been resting. "I *want* you, Randy Hayes," he snarled. "What do you think of *that*!"

Miranda drew in her breath and faced him boldly. "I think that whatever you want to do to me, you will. After all, you're stronger than I am. Just don't take me like your father would take a woman, Jake. And don't do it just to try to scare me off, because you can't. I love you, Jake Harkner, and you damn well know it! You'd never hurt me!" Unwanted tears suddenly filled her eyes, and she felt his grip relax. He massaged her arms for a moment.

"Damn you, woman," he said softly then. "How do you know me that well?" He leaned closer, kissed her eyes, licked at her tears, found her mouth and licked at that too. Miranda found that her instinctive response to him was powerful, as though it was always supposed to be this way. She closed her eyes and met his tongue, letting him slake his own between her lips in a kiss more delicious than any kiss Mack had ever given her. Had she just been too young then to fully enjoy a man? Or perhaps she had just been too long without. She only knew this felt more wonderful than anything she had ever experienced.

Jake groaned, and his kiss grew hotter, deeper. She felt him pull a few blankets down, let him lay her down on them. Never had she wanted a man like this, with such wantonness, such an agonizing need. She returned his kisses with a fiery passion she had not known she was capable of feeling.

THE LAST HIGHWAYMAN
by
Katherine O'Neal

We are proud to publish the first historical romance by a truly exciting new voice in women's fiction!

Christina left home at sixteen to escape her parents—stars of the English theatre who exploited her brilliance as a costume designer and makeup artist, but never forgave their daughter for surviving a flu epidemic in which her twin sister died. Best friends with the wicked Oscar Wilde, and married young to an aged duke who died soon after, she has money, power, and position—but she has never known reckless passion . . . never found enduring love.

Richard is the dangerously handsome son of a Lord who married a beautiful Irish girl only to offer her to the licentious Prince of Wales in exchange for wealth and power. Sworn to avenge his mother's fate and aid the Irish rebellion against the crown, he expects only ransom when he abducts the beautiful outspoken duchess from her bedroom late one night. Instead, he finds he has captured a woman who will become known as "the bandit's bride"—a woman strong enough to heal his tormented soul, and so dazzlingly seductive in his arms she will possess his heart forever.

THE LAST HIGHWAYMAN is a delectable action-packed novel of irresistible romance and fascinating history, highly emotional and full of witty dialogue and unexpected twists.

"Going somewhere, Duchess?" the Captain asked.

She backed up against the stone wall of the forge, but he followed, keeping the sharp blade perched against her neck. He was so close that she could feel the hard contours of his body pressing into hers. Her breath was coming fast now as her mind raced. She could outsmart him, but she couldn't overpower him.

"How did you know I'd try to escape?" she gasped.

"A number of ways. You never asked why I kept you here, or for how long. I've never once known a woman who wasn't curious about her fate."

Damn! She hadn't thought of that. She lifted her chin with a show of bravado. "Well?" she demanded. "Are you going to slash my throat? Cut off my ear?"

He ran the knife along her neck in a ruminative manner. "Frankly, I can think of more interesting things to cut."

His voice was at her ear, muffled and intimate, yet hard as steel. Putting a thumb to her throat, he moved the knife and cut away the top button of her riding habit. She shivered. In the distance, she heard the men heading back for the mill. She took a breath to cry out, but he pressed himself against her in a menacing way.

"I wouldn't. They'd just assume that I was doing what I'm doing, and leave me to my spoils."

She was shaking uncontrollably. "You won't like it," she warned in a croaking voice. "I'm dead inside. I can no longer feel anything. You might as well vent your lust on a sack of meal."

He cut away the second button. "Is that why you spent last night vexing me? To show how impervious you are to desire?"

"I merely meant to distract you, to keep your mind from my escape."

He cut away the third button, opened the bodice with the point of his knife, and lowered his lips to her neck. "You did a fine job of—distracting me, I must say."

She found courage enough to taunt him. "I've over-estimated you. I wouldn't think a man like you would have to resort to rape. You disappoint me, highwayman."

He ignored her. One by one, the buttons were severed to fall on the stone floor. He undressed her slowly, as if he had all the time in the world, tossing each piece of her clothing aside.

When she was naked, he turned her so that her back was to him. He rested his left arm around the front of her shoulders so that the knife once again lay across the hollow of her throat.

Bending, he kissed her shoulder, felt her shiver against the night air. With his right hand, he stroked her belly and moved up to cup the mound of her breast. She swayed and her breath became labored.

"You're a weak-livered coward," she moaned, "forcing your attentions on women who have no interest."

His hand moved to the other breast.

"I should die of shame, knowing I had to force a woman at the point of a knife," she continued.

He brought his lips to her ear. Her breath caught in her throat as he nuzzled the side of her neck.

"I wouldn't have you if you were the last man—"

He trailed his hand along her belly and down a path to her thigh.

"Weak, despicable cad," she accused, but her voice was breathless now.

Against her will, she leaned back into him, conforming her body to his. She rubbed against him like a cat against a post.

Finally he spoke. His mouth was at her ear and his voice was deep and hushed, yet ruthlessly hard. "I've never raped a woman in my life," he informed her, his breath warming her ear. "I have no intention of starting now."

"You make a poor showing of your good intentions," she retorted in a voice crackling with passion.

"I shall give you nothing you don't ask for voluntarily. So you see, my lady, the game is up to you."

Having stated his intentions, his mouth moved once again to her shoulder. He kissed the satiny skin, making his way with infinite leisure down the quivering flesh of her arm. His hands explored her body with feathery strokes as he awaited her reply.

She sighed and dropped her head back against him. "Put your knife away, highwayman," she directed. "You'll have no need of it this night."

He was still. Then, removing the blade from her throat, he tossed the weapon into the half-roof so that it landed in a far beam with a twang.

Freed, she pivoted around and began to unbutton his shirt. "Your grace! You shock me!" he mocked.

"I'm an impatient woman, highwayman. It takes more than weapons and promises to satisfy me."

Stepping out of his boots, he asked, "Have you ever been satisfied?"

She showed her teeth in a wicked smile. "Never."

"You are about," he informed her, "to put that in the past tense."

She gave him a lusty chuckle. "Well,"—she shrugged—"I admire your confidence. You are, most certainly, welcome to try."

Any other man might have been intimidated by her challenge. He showed no sign of such quaverings. Taking her shoulders in his hands, he pulled her to him very slowly, so that her breasts just barely touched his chest, until—slowly, slowly—she could feel every rigid contour of his frame.

He kissed her with the same exquisite languor. His lips were firm, and they moved over hers with practised ease. She'd expected rape. What he was giving her was seduction. He seemed to be moving in slow motion, luxuriating in each touch, each kiss, each moan of pleasure that escaped her throat. As his hands stroked her body, igniting the long-dormant flames, he tasted of her mouth with a leisure that was devastating.

Soon, it became unbearable. Her body, denied since the ravages of the Prince, was alive with passion, with hunger, with need. She pressed herself against him, urging him on . . .

CONFIDENCES
by
Penny Hayden

In the bestselling tradition of Danielle Steel, CONFIDENCES is a warm, deeply moving novel about four "thirty-something" mothers, whose lives are interwoven by a long-held secret—a secret that could now save the life of a seventeen-year-old boy dying of leukemia.

When Douglass Summers discovers that he needs a bone marrow transplant, his parents are forced to admit that he was adopted. It is his desperate search for his biological mother and father that triggers the compelling stories of four very different women who are the closest of friends, yet who have something important to discover about themselves as mothers—and as women. Their separate trials and struggles for love and passion are powerfully portrayed in this wise, poignant novel that captures all the drama and complexities of modern love.

July

San Francisco

It wasn't anyone's fault. At least that was what Mom and Dad and his doctor kept telling him. It wasn't his fault; it wasn't his parents' fault; there wasn't a damn thing to blame except some stupid cells gone crazy.

Turning his face toward the hospital room window, Doug Sommers blinked hard to keep back the tears stinging his eyes. He wished everyone would leave so he could cry instead of having to act so goddamn brave all over the place. He was only seventeen, for Christ's sake. He didn't want to die.

While Dr. Levison droned on to Mom and Dad about white

blood cells and platelets and chemotherapy and bone marrow, Doug aimed the remote control at the television and zapped it on, then flicked through the channels until he found MTV. By the time he got out of the hospital, summer would be over, school would have started, and there'd be a whole new bunch of songs on the top-ten list.

Some senior year. Instead of playing football, he'd be taking a mess of drugs that would make him feel even worse than he did now; instead of going out with Jennifer, he'd be getting stuck with needles and his blond hair would be falling out in handfuls. He'd read *Brian's Song* in seventh grade—he knew what to expect: first they tortured you; then you died. He poked a button on the control, and the television clicked off.

"So, how does that sound, Doug?" Dr. Levison's voice was low and pleasant, but direct, not at all syrupy like those doctors who went around saying, "And how are we feeling today?" He had to hand it to her; at least she was honest. She smiled at him as if she expected him to be pleased by whatever it was she'd been telling his parents.

It was easy for her. She wasn't going to die before she'd ever really lived. He shrugged, his grip tightening on the remote control as he fought the urge to heave it at the window. All he wanted to do right now was scream and cry and break things. But every time he looked at Mom and Dad, at the love and grief engraved on their faces, he tensed against the horrible rage twisting his guts, invading his blood like the malignant myeloid cells the tests had discovered. It wasn't their fault, he reminded himself again, for the hundredth time. He had to keep it together for them.

"I'm sorry," he said. "I sort of spaced out."

"I was just explaining to your parents what doctors call a *protocol*, what I think is the best treatment plan for you. The first goal is to get you into remission." Dr. Levison nodded at his parents. "That's accomplished through induction therapy—or chemotherapy, in your case. At this point we may not need to resort to radiotherapy."

"Then I won't lose my hair?" His face flushed as soon as the words were out. What the hell did it matter if he was bald when he died?

"Some drugs may make it a little thinner, but, no, you

probably won't lose it all." Her tone was serious, matter-of-fact, as if he'd asked a perfectly reasonable question. "There are a number of other possible side effects of the drugs we use to induce remission. But if we're successful, there's the possibility of a bone marrow transplant, where we replace your diseased marrow with a donor's healthy marrow. It's still experimental, but the overall results have been good, and some transplant patients are still in remission after more than eight years. I was just going to explain it to your parents. Should I come back later or are you ready to hear about it now?"

His cheeks grew even hotter. She seemed to understand how angry he was, and she didn't seem to mind at all. "I guess so," he mumbled, laying the control on the bedside table. He spread his hands out over the white covers and stared at them. Maybe it wasn't so helpless after all. Suddenly, eight years looked like a lifetime. He could do a lot in eight years—finish high school, graduate from college, maybe even get married. At the very least, he wouldn't die a virgin; he'd make damn sure of that.

"You have a lot of points in your favor," she said. "You're young; your general physical condition is excellent; your internal organs appear to be in good shape; you've never been treated for blood cell diseases before." She turned to his parents. "The biggest consideration in bone marrow transplants, however, is finding a prospective donor, someone with a matching HL-A type. We find that out by testing the lymphocytes in the blood to see if they share the same antigens and by culturing the donor's blood with the patient's to see if the cells attack each other." She smiled at Doug. "You have two younger brothers, right?"

"Yeah." He pushed himself up straighter and cocked his head, the warmth of hope loosening the constricted, cold feeling in his chest. "But what have they got to do with it?"

"Well, an identical twin would be ideal because he would have the same chromosomal inheritance as you. But since you don't have a twin, we'll look at your brothers. Genetically speaking, there's a 25 percent chance for each one to be a good match. Parents are a possibility, too, though the chances are much slimmer."

Doug's mother drew her breath in sharply and glanced at his father. "Genetically?" she whispered, then cleared her throat.

Dr. Levison raised a dark eyebrow and looked back and forth from his mother to his father. "Is that a problem?"

For the first time during the two days since the blood tests for his football physical had shown there was something wrong, Mom's eyes filled with tears. She opened her mouth to speak, but no words came out. Finally, she buried her face in her hands.

Dad put an arm around her shoulder and pulled her close. He shook his head slowly, then touched Dr. Levison's shoulder. "May we have a few minutes alone with Doug?"

"Certainly," she said. "I'll be at the nurses' station."

Even though the room was silent after she left, Doug's ears buzzed. Mom and Dad had been so calm about everything. Until now. He took a deep breath of the disinfectant-laden air, then broke the silence. "What's up?" he said, pushing his lips into something he hoped resembled a smile. "First good news I've heard, and you guys—"

Mom's hands dropped to her side, and she lifted her head. Tears streamed down her cheeks, and she clenched her teeth. "We meant to tell you a long time ago, but somehow—" Her voice broke. "We love you so much. It never made any difference, not even after your brothers were born?"

Bitter-tasting saliva flooded Doug's mouth. "*What* never made any difference?"

Dad sucked in a deep breath. "We adopted you when you were a week old. We have no idea who your biological parents are."

OFFICIAL RULES TO WINNERS CLASSIC SWEEPSTAKES

No Purchase necessary. To enter the sweepstakes follow instructions found elsewhere in this offer. You can also enter the sweepstakes by hand printing your name, address, city, state and zip code on a 3" x 5" piece of paper and mailing it to: Winners Classic Sweepstakes, P.O. Box 785, Gibbstown, NJ 08027. Mail each entry separately. Sweepstakes begins 12/1/91. Entries must be received by 6/1/93. Some presentations of this sweepstakes may feature a deadline for the Early Bird prize. If the offer you receive does, then to be eligible for the Early Bird prize your entry must be received according to the Early Bird date specified. Not responsible for lost, late, damaged, misdirected, illegible or postage due mail. Mechanically reproduced entries are not eligible. All entries become property of the sponsor and will not be returned.

Prize Selection/Validations: Winners will be selected in random drawings on or about 7/30/93, by VENTURA ASSOCIATES, INC., an independent judging organization whose decisions are final. Odds of winning are determined by total number of entries received. Circulation of this sweepstakes is estimated not to exceed 200 million. Entrants need not be present to win. All prizes are guaranteed to be awarded and delivered to winners. Winners will be notified by mail and may be required to complete an affidavit of eligibility and release of liability which must be returned within 14 days of date of notification or alternate winners will be selected. Any guest of a trip winner will also be required to execute a release of liability. Any prize notification letter or any prize returned to a participating sponsor, Bantam Doubleday Dell Publishing Group, Inc., its participating divisions or subsidiaries, or VENTURA ASSOCIATES, INC. as undeliverable will be awarded to an alternate winner. Prizes are not transferable. No multiple prize winners except as may be necessary due to unavailability, in which case a prize of equal or greater value will be awarded. Prizes will be awarded approximately 90 days after the drawing. All taxes, automobile license and registration fees, if applicable, are the sole responsibility of the winners. Entry constitutes permission (except where prohibited) to use winners' names and likenesses for publicity purposes without further or other compensation.

Participation: This sweepstakes is open to residents of the United States and Canada, except for the province of Quebec. This sweepstakes is sponsored by Bantam Doubleday Dell Publishing Group, Inc. (BDD), 666 Fifth Avenue, New York, NY 10103. Versions of this sweepstakes with different graphics will be offered in conjunction with various solicitations or promotions by different subsidiaries and divisions of BDD. Employees and their families of BDD, its division, subsidiaries, advertising agencies, and VENTURA ASSOCIATES, INC., are not eligible.

Canadian residents, in order to win, must first correctly answer a time limited arithmetical skill testing question. Void in Quebec and wherever prohibited or restricted by law. Subject to all federal, state, local and provincial laws and regulations.

Prizes: The following values for prizes are determined by the manufacturers' suggested retail prices or by what these items are currently known to be selling for at the time this offer was published. Approximate retail values include handling and delivery of prizes. Estimated maximum retail value of prizes: 1 Grand Prize ($27,500 if merchandise or $25,000 Cash); 1 First Prize ($3,000); 5 Second Prizes ($400 each); 35 Third Prizes ($100 each); 1,000 Fourth Prizes ($9.00 each) ; 1 Early Bird Prize ($5,000); Total approximate maximum retail value is $50,000. Winners will have the option of selecting any prize offered at level won. Automobile winner must have a valid driver's license at the time the car is awarded. Trips are subject to space and departure availability. Certain black-out dates may apply. Travel must be completed within one year from the time the prize is awarded. Minors must be accompanied by an adult. Prizes won by minors will be awarded in the name of parent or legal guardian.

For a list of Major Prize Winners (available after 7/30/93): send a self-addressed, stamped envelope entirely separate from your entry to: Winners Classic Sweepstakes Winners, P.O. Box 825, Gibbstown, NJ 08027. Requests must be received by 6/1/93. DO NOT SEND ANY OTHER CORRESPONDENCE TO THIS P.O. BOX.

Women's Fiction

On Sale in February

TEMPERATURES RISING

56045-X $5.99/6.99 in Canada

☐ **by Sandra Brown**

New York Times bestselling author of
A WHOLE NEW LIGHT and FRENCH SILK

A contemporary tale of love and passion in the South Pacific.

OUTLAW HEARTS

29807-0 $5.99/6.99 in Canada

☐ **by Rosanne Bittner**

Bestselling author of SONG OF THE WOLF,
praised by *Romantic Times* as "a stunning
achievement...that moves the soul and fills the heart."

THE LAST HIGHWAYMAN

56065-4 $5.50/6.50 in Canada

☐ **by Katherine O'Neal**

Fascinating historical fact and sizzling romantic fiction meet
in this sensual tale of a legendary bandit and a scandalous
high-born lady.

CONFIDENCES

56170-7 $4.99/5.99 in Canada

☐ **by Penny Hayden**

"Thirtysomething" meets Danielle Steel—four best friends
are bound by an explosive secret.

Ask for these books at your local bookstore or use this page to order.

☐ Please send me the books I have checked above. I am enclosing $ _____ (add $2.50
to cover postage and handling). Send check or money order, no cash or C. O. D.'s please.

Name _____

Address _____

City/ State/ Zip _____

Send order to: Bantam Books, Dept. FN95, 2451 S. Wolf Rd., Des Plaines, IL 60018
Allow four to six weeks for delivery.
Prices and availability subject to change without notice.

FN95 3/93

Women's Fiction

On Sale in March

ONCE AN ANGEL

☐ 29409-1 $5.50/6.50 in Canada
by Teresa Medeiros
Bestselling author of HEATHER AND VELVET

A captivating historical romance that sweeps from the wilds of an exotic paradise to the elegance of Victorian England.
"Teresa Medeiros writes rare love stories to cherish."
— Romantic Times

IN A ROGUE'S ARMS

☐ 29692-2 $4.99/5.99 in Canada
by Virginia Brown writing as Virginia Lynn
Author of LYON'S PRIZE

A passion-filled retelling of the beloved Robin Hood tale, set in Texas of the 1870's. The first of Bantam's new "Once Upon a Time" romances: passionate historical romances with themes from fairy tales, myths, and legends.

THE LADY AND THE CHAMP

☐ 29655-8 $4.99/5.99 in Canada
by Fran Baker

Bestselling Loveswept author Fran Baker's first mainstream romance! The passionate story of a boxer/lawyer and the interior decorator who inherited his gym — and won his heart.
"Unforgettable...a warm, wonderful knockout of a book."
— Julie Garwood

Bestselling Women's Fiction

Sandra Brown

_____	29783-X A WHOLE NEW LIGHT	$5.99/6.99 in Canada
_____	29500-4 TEXAS! SAGE	$5.99/6.99
_____	29085-1 22 INDIGO PLACE	$4.50/5.50
_____	28990-X TEXAS! CHASE	$5.99/6.99
_____	28951-9 TEXAS! LUCKY	$5.99/6.99

Amanda Quick

_____	29316-8 RAVISHED	$4.99/5.99
_____	29315-X RECKLESS	$5.99/6.99
_____	29325-7 RENDEZVOUS	$4.99/5.99
_____	28932-2 SCANDAL	$4.95/5.95
_____	28354-5 SEDUCTION	$4.99/5.99
_____	28594-7 SURRENDER	$5.99/6.99

Nora Roberts

_____	29490-3 DIVINE EVIL	$5.99/6.99
_____	29597-7 CARNAL INNOCENCE	$5.50/6.50
_____	29078-9 GENUINE LIES	$4.99/5.99
_____	28578-5 PUBLIC SECRETS	$4.95/5.95
_____	26461-3 HOT ICE	$4.99/5.99
_____	26574-1 SACRED SINS	$5.50/6.50
_____	27859-2 SWEET REVENGE	$5.50/6.50
_____	27283-7 BRAZEN VIRTUE	$4.99/5.99

Iris Johansen

_____	29968-9 THE TIGER PRINCE	$5.50/6.50
_____	29871-2 LAST BRIDGE HOME	$4.50/5.50
_____	29604-3 THE GOLDEN BARBARIAN	$4.99/5.99
_____	29244-7 REAP THE WIND	$4.99/5.99
_____	29032-0 STORM WINDS	$4.99/5.99
_____	28855-5 THE WIND DANCER	$4.95/5.95

Ask for these titles at your bookstore or use this page to order.